Ravenous want made Kellen crazy for...

The way he regarded her set her blood aflame.

When he ran a tongue over his fangs and gazed down at her, Sophie could hardly catch her breath. Closing his eyes, he pressed his nose to her and inhaled her scent.

Like a gentle breeze, his hands swept over her, careful not to touch too much too soon.

She itched to ease her own suffering. But she couldn't. Kellen wouldn't let her. She was at his mercy. And she liked it.

Books by Vivi Anna

VIVI ANNA

A vixen at heart, Vivi Anna likes to burn up the pages with her unique brand of fantasy fiction. Whether it's in the Amazon jungle, an apocalyptic future or the otherworld city of Necropolis, Vivi always writes fast-paced action-adventure with strong, independent women and dark, delicious heroes.

Once shot at while repossessing a car, Vivi decided that maybe her life needed a change. The first time she picked up a pen and put words to paper, she knew she had found her heart's desire. Within two paragraphs, she realized she could write about getting into all sorts of trouble without suffering any of the consequences.

When Vivi isn't writing, you can find her causing a ruckus at downtown bistros, flea markets or in her own backyard.

THE
VAMPIRE'S QUEST
VIVI ANNA

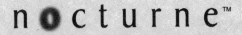

Silhouette® Books

nocturne™

If you purchased this book without a cover you should be aware
that this book is stolen property. It was reported as "unsold and
destroyed" to the publisher, and neither the author nor the
publisher has received any payment for this "stripped book."

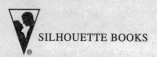 SILHOUETTE BOOKS

ISBN-13: 978-0-373-61808-8
ISBN-10:   0-373-61808-5

Recycling programs
for this product may
not exist in your area.

THE VAMPIRE'S QUEST

Copyright © 2009 by Tawny Stokes

All rights reserved. Except for use in any review, the reproduction
or utilization of this work in whole or in part in any form by any
electronic, mechanical or other means, now known or hereafter
invented, including xerography, photocopying and recording, or in
any information storage or retrieval system, is forbidden without
the written permission of the editorial office, Silhouette Books,
233 Broadway, New York, NY 10279 U.S.A.

This is a work of fiction. Names, characters, places and incidents are
either the product of the author's imagination or are used fictitiously, and
any resemblance to actual persons, living or dead, business establishments,
events or locales is entirely coincidental.

This edition published by arrangement with Harlequin Books S.A.

® and TM are trademarks of Harlequin Books S.A., used under license.
Trademarks indicated with ® are registered in the United States Patent
and Trademark Office, the Canadian Trade Marks Office and in other
countries.

www.silhouettenocturne.com

Printed in U.S.A.

Dear Reader,

Ever since the first book in the VALORIAN CHRONICLES, *Blood Secrets*, came out, I have received a ton of e-mails asking for Kellen Falcon's story. So I am thrilled to be able to give it to you now.

I don't know what it is about him—it could be his unconventional looks and attitude, his carefree spirit or the fact that women love a bad boy—but Kellen, since his first appearance, has continually been a standout character for me and, obviously, for you.

Because of this, I had to write a different type of story for him. So buckle in and hang on as we fly away across the ocean to another city—the progressive otherworld city of Nouveau Monde, where Kellen will find everything he never knew he was looking for.

Happy reading!

Vivi Anna

Come visit me at www.vivianna.net for excerpts of my other books and contests.

For Mom and Dad, because without you...
well, you know the rest....

Chapter 1

The orchestra music playing in the elevator, as it ascended to the ninth floor of the Nouveau Monde medical center, was driving Kellen Falcon mad. Or maybe it was the disease rushing through his veins that had finally pushed him over the edge.

The other people in the elevator must have noticed his growing agitation, since they were pressed against the walls, away from him. It couldn't possibly be his appearance anymore. He ran a hand through his newly grown-in brown hair. It was quite a change from his usual bald pate. All his piercings were gone; his body couldn't tolerate the metal invasion any longer.

He looked just like everyone else now. Sometimes he

had to admit that looking in the mirror surprised him. Gone was the crazy-looking vampire with issues. His recently acquired blood disorder had taken care of all that.

He'd only been in the Otherworlder European city for five days now, but it was enough for the culture shock to grate on his nerves. Usually a carefree, whatever-makes-you-happy kind of guy, Kellen found the laid-back, meandering quality of the city strangely annoying. Even the quaint architecture and cobblestone streets bothered him. Walking out from his small rented room in the picturesque downtown square, he'd expected horses and buggies ambling down the old-world, narrow roads. Maybe it was because he was used to the constant rush of living in America.

Or his *Sangcerritus* was getting progressively worse—the reason he was in Nouveau Monde.

After being diagnosed with the rare blood disease months ago, Kellen had conducted a lot of research and found that there were a couple of doctors who were leading experts on it—and one of the doctors lived in Nouveau Monde. There had even been talk of a possible cure.

He didn't dare hope for that much. He was merely looking for a way to alleviate the symptoms so he could lead some semblance of an ordinary life again. Or as ordinary as a one-hundred-and-eighty-year-old vampire could get.

The elevator dinged pleasantly, announcing its

arrival at the ninth floor, and the doors slid open. Kellen stepped out into a lavishly decorated lobby welcoming people to the hematology department. The effect was lost on him. A young, impeccably dressed woman sat at the impressive semicircular, raised platform desk, smiling and nodding to people as they passed by.

When he neared, she smiled brightly, the white of her descended fangs nearly blinding him. *"Bonsoir. Peux-je vous aider?"*

"Bonsoir. I'm looking for Dr. Bueller's office."

She gestured to Kellen's left. "His office is just down this hall, second door on the right," she said in accented English.

She smiled again, and this time there was a gleam in her beautiful green eyes. An invitation. On another day, in what seemed a lifetime ago, he would have been interested in what the alluring French woman offered. But now, given his circumstance, he just wanted to live. The clock was ticking loudly in his mind.

"Merci," he said, then made his way down the hall.

Opening the second door, he was again greeted by a huge lobby area, this one announcing the offices of Dr. Jonathon Bueller. Another young woman sat at the reception desk, grinning as he approached. The big difference here was that she was human, which surprised him.

He wasn't quite used to the idea that humans and Otherworlders lived in relative peace and harmony in Nouveau Monde. He'd almost jumped out of his skin the first time he'd seen a human walking down the street near his hotel, hand in hand with a lycan. Even to someone as out of place as he was, the coupling was strange.

"Bonsoir."

He nodded. "Kellen Falcon to see Dr. Bueller."

She glanced at her computer screen, typed something, then looked back at him, handing him a clipboard with a form attached to it. "If you would, have a seat and fill this out."

Kellen took the clipboard and sat down in the far corner, near the floor-to-ceiling windows that overlooked the impressive Seine River. While he filled out the detailed form, he periodically glanced through the glass at the vivid green park running along the riverbank. The evening shadows were playing along the edges, reminding him of puppets on strings.

Nouveau Monde was certainly beautiful, with its lush park areas and old-world charm. Having grown up in New Orleans circa the early 1800s, he'd been surrounded by French culture and styles his whole life. So a few sexy accents and architectural gems didn't sway him much.

But still, there was something about the place that resonated in him. The fact that humans lived and worked in and around the city interested him. It was a striking difference between here and Necropolis, where the Otherworlders were caged like inmates, and the humans on the outside cowered in fear and ignorance. Europe had always been more progressive and ahead of the times. His kind of place.

He'd also heard from the gentleman he rented the room from that the nightlife in the city was spectacular. He didn't know if he'd feel up to going to clubs, although he sure could use a few drinks to try to relax. He'd been craving a distraction for months now. He'd yet to find one.

After completing the form, he handed it back to the receptionist, then sat back down to wait for his appointment. There were five other people in the waiting room, all vampires, save for one out-of-place lycan. Kellen wondered what kind of blood disease he had. He didn't think lycans could contract diseases.

Thinking about lycans made him nostalgic about Necropolis and the Otherworld Crime Unit he'd worked with for the past six years. After being diagnosed with the disease, he had applied for an openended leave of absence and booked a flight to France. He didn't think any of the team missed him too much; the last year hadn't been his best. On a few occasions he'd come head-to-head with various members of the team, especially the chief, Caine Valorian.

They hadn't known about his disease—why he was constantly grumpy, and lashing out. Then again, neither had he at the time. He thought that his irritation had been caused by the fact that most of the *team members* were irritating.

Once his problem was under control, he wondered if he'd be able to return to work with them. Leaning back in the chair and glancing out the window at the darkening indigo sky, Kellen considered the thought that maybe he didn't want to. He bet he could find work here with little effort. He certainly didn't need the money, as he'd amassed enough over the past one hundred years. Maybe a change in scenery was what he needed to heal, to get his life back on track—instead of just existing from one day to the next.

A few bars of a hard-core metal song thumped from his jeans pocket. He fished out his cell phone and flipped it open. "Falcon."

"How's Europe? Are they trying to deport you yet?"

Kellen smirked at the humor in Caine's voice. The chief was usually not one for jokes. "Not yet. Give me a few more days."

Caine's unexpected chuckle suddenly made him feel homesick.

"Monsieur. Monsieur."

Kellen glanced at the receptionist. She was motioning to him with a wave of her pen.

"Hold on, Caine." He put his hand over the phone. "Yeah?"

"No cell phones, please." She pointed to the sign by her desk, the one with a big red *X* over a picture of a cell phone.

Waving that he understood, Kellen stood and wandered out of the office and down the hall, then said into the phone, "Are you still there?"

"Yes. What happened? Did you get kicked out of somewhere?"

"Yeah, my doctor's office. I guess they don't like cell phones around all the electrical equipment."

The vampiress at the main reception desk smiled at him as he leaned against the wall near her. He nodded at her.

"How's it going?"

Kellen appreciated Caine's query about his health. They hadn't parted on the best of terms after Caine had accused him of blowing up the lab. "It's my first appointment. I'll know more after I talk to this guy."

"Okay. You'll call when you find out?"

"Yeah." He ran a hand over his head, feeling strange about Caine's concern. Not exactly good friends, Kellen could count on one hand the number of times they'd ever engaged in a personal conversation. But he had to admit, he liked that the chief had called. It made him feel a little less alone.

Static filled his ear. Pushing away from the wall, Kellen turned the phone in his hand. "Caine?"

"Yeah, I'm here. I can barely hear you, though." More static crackled through the line.

"There's a lot of interference in here. I'll call you later." Kellen flipped his phone closed and slid it into his pants pocket.

A loud, piercing, shrill sound echoed from the doctor's office down the hall. Everyone in the reception area looked up at the strident noise.

"Looks like someone else didn't turn their phone off," Kellen said to the receptionist.

She smiled at him, and then went back to her keyboard.

He glanced at his watch. He still had five minutes to kill before his appointment. He squinted down at the watch face. Something was wrong with it.

The second hand seemed to have stopped. He tapped the plastic covering. No, it hadn't stopped, but it was barely moving, as if suspended in some kind of liquid. Looking up, he noticed that other things in the lobby were off.

The clock on the wall over the receptionist's desk displayed the same effect as his watch. Even the vampiress seemed to be moving more slowly. Her actions and reactions to things were about a second off in time. There was a blur of motion over her body. Like when a photograph is out of focus.

The hair on his arms rose. A multitude of heartbeats from everyone on the floor thundered in his ears, making him wince. All of them were in sync.

Thump.

Thump.

Thump.

All except for one. He recognized that ticking for what it was.

In a blink of an eye, he crossed the distance between him and the receptionist. Grabbing her around the waist, he brought her down to the ground and covered her with his body.

The sound of her scream was the last thing he heard before everything around them exploded.

Chapter 2

The ringing in his ears was deafening. Leaning forward in the chair he was seated in, Kellen put his head in his hands to try and dampen the discordant noise. He was dizzy, and it was making him sick. His stomach roiled in protest.

He tried to focus on what the uniformed officer standing in front of him was saying, but it sounded like mumbled nonsense. He couldn't concentrate on anything but the body bags being carried out from the demolished medical offices. Three of them lined one end of the foyer.

The only other survivor that he could see was the receptionist. She was strapped to a stretcher, with an oxygen mask on her face. Another officer was standing alongside with an open notebook, trying to ask her questions. She didn't look as if she was in any shape to talk, let alone answer any queries about what had happened. *He* didn't even know, and he was at least coherent. Mostly.

Blinking at the officer, Kellen shook his head and grabbed the man's arm. "I can't understand what you're saying. Can you write it down?" Even his own voice sounded muffled, as if coming through water.

The officer glanced over his shoulder at another man roaming the scene with an open notepad and pen in his mouth—a plainclothes officer dressed in dark jeans, blazer and tie. He waved the man over.

As the new cop approached Kellen, he could feel the man probing him with his intense stare. The man's power wasn't vampiric, though. It wasn't strictly lycan, either. He had the same swagger that most lycans possess. Confident and sturdy, with an understated intelligence that most people missed. Kellen was not most people. He knew the look of a clever predator—from one to another.

The plainclothes officer grabbed a chair and set it beside Kellen, settling himself into it with an air of casual indifference. He leaned back and set his notepad on his lap.

"I'm Inspector Gabriel Bellmonte."

There was something in his voice that pushed aside the other interfering noises in Kellen's ear, stabilizing the spinning in his mind. Kellen heard the man clearly. He'd never heard of a lycan possessing that kind of power.

"Kellen Falcon."

"I know who you are, Monsieur Falcon. Caine Valorian informed me that you would be in my city." *My* city. Kellen didn't need extrasensory hearing to understand that message. "What were you doing here?"

"I had an appointment with Dr. Bueller."

"What time was your appointment?"

"Seven o'clock."

"How many people did you see in the office?"

"Five, four vampires and a lycan, and the human receptionist. Which I found odd."

"There are quite a few humans in Nouveau Monde. We work together instead of fight, like in America."

Kellen heard the disdain in the inspector's voice. It was obvious he didn't think too highly of Otherworld Americans.

Gabriel wrote in his notebook. "Did you notice anything out of the ordinary right before the explosion?"

Kellen told the inspector about talking on his cell phone in the main lobby, his watch, the time shift and the other cell phone ringing from Dr. Bueller's office right before the blast.

"Lucky for you that you were out here in the main lobby and not in the other office."

"Was it a bomb?" Kellen asked.

"We don't know yet. There have been some previous electrical problems in this building, so we're not ruling out anything at this point."

Gabriel flipped his notebook closed. "The receptionist told me that you grabbed her and threw her to the floor right before the explosion." He arched a brow. He didn't need to say the words; Kellen knew exactly what he was asking.

"I have an affinity for the incendiary," he joked, but the inspector didn't smile, so he tried again. "I felt the shock waves before they happened."

The inspector nodded and stood. "That's an interesting gift you have there, Monsieur Falcon, to know when an explosion is going to happen."

"No more interesting than a lycan who can power-speak like a vampire."

Gabriel laughed as he shoved his notepad and pen into his jacket pocket. "Ah, but I have my great-grandfather's bloodline on my side. He was a powerful vampire. What's your excuse?"

Kellen shrugged. "Just lucky, I suppose."

"I don't have to tell you not to leave town any time soon, do I?"

"You just did." Kellen smiled grimly. Although the lycan was cavalier in a self-important kind of way, he liked him. "Besides, I'm hoping to reschedule that appointment with the doctor."

Gabriel narrowed his eyes. "Hmm, well, let's hope the good doctor is one of the survivors like you, then."

Kellen heard the derision in the inspector's voice. It was time to cut his losses while he still could. He'd never been one to get along with law enforcement. Even working with them side-by-side for so many years was a lesson in futility—mostly for them.

"Do you have any more questions? My head is killing me. I'd love to go back to my hotel room and drown my pain in a bottle of vodka."

"Give me just a few more minutes, then I'll have a uniform drive you to your hotel."

Kellen rubbed at his right ear, trying to dislodge the painful ringing. "You could just ask me where I'm staying. It would be easier." His ear finally popped and he could hear again.

The inspector's brow furrowed. "Yes, but for whom?"

Kellen watched Bellmonte, as he wandered back to the explosion site and the neat row of body bags. The row was getting longer. Two attendants carried another gray plastic bag out from the destroyed room. Following them were two crime scene techs in dark-blue nylon jackets. Both women.

One was a vampire, a strong one by the power waves she was emitting, and the other wasn't. A witch, perhaps. Lycan possibly, by the graceful way she moved.

Gabriel crouched next to the bag, and after putting on a glove, he unzipped the bag and winced.

"Most of him is in there," one of the crime scene techs, the vampiress, said. Her voice was heavily accented, Kellen noticed, maybe French-Russian. "A foot and a few fingers are missing. We'll find them in the cleanup."

"Any ID?"

The other tech, a stunning redhead, handed Gabriel a piece of burnt plastic. The inspector rubbed at the soot with his gloved thumb. "Dr. Bueller."

The inspector glanced over his shoulder at Kellen. The crime-scene techs followed suit. He raised the identifying piece of plastic. "Looks like you won't be rescheduling that appointment."

Sighing, Kellen rubbed a hand over his face. It didn't surprise him that the doctor was dead. It was just his kind of luck.

The Russian tech's full mouth tilted up, not quite into a smile, but close. She had an air of seduction around her. He had a sneaky suspicion that that was her particular specialty. Most vampires had special powers. Some could hypnotize with their eyes, others with their voice. Caine Valorian could detect emotion, any emotion, from a smell or taste. He was one man Kellen couldn't lie to, even if he wanted to. This vampiress seemed to possess a powerful ability to seduce. But it wasn't working on him.

The other one, the redhead, aimed a gorgeous, blue-eyed gaze that pinned him where he sat. If the Russian was fire, this one was all ice, despite the fiery color of her hair. It was too bad really, because there was something about her that made his gut twist into a knot.

After what seemed like an eternity, she finally turned and went back to the main crime scene. He watched as she walked away, appreciating the way her khaki pants fit over her long legs and curvy behind. She had a confident stride. She was a lycan for sure.

His view became obstructed by a uniformed police officer, the same one who had spoken to him earlier. "I am to take you to your hotel now."

Warily, Kellen pushed to his feet and followed the officer across the main floor foyer to the stairwell exit. As he walked, Gabriel watched him, a pensive look on his face. The vampiress watched him, too, but her look was anything but pensive.

When he reached the door, the inspector nodded in his direction. "I'll be in touch."

The statement was innocuous enough, but Kellen felt a bit of force behind the words, especially with the way the inspector was regarding him—as if Kellen was his number-one suspect.

Chapter 3

After another three hours at the crime scene picking up pieces, literally, of the victims and the medical office, Sophie St. Clair was exhausted. Running on only a few hours of sleep to begin with, she'd been nearly ready to fall asleep on her feet when she got the call about the explosion.

That was until she'd felt the vampire's gaze on her. That had woken her up. Now her whole body was on edge.

Sipping a strong cup of coffee, she settled into her chair and fired up the computer. The first thing she needed to check on was any mechanical or electrical problems that had been addressed at the medical center over the past year. The team had to determine whether this was accidental or intentional. She really hoped for the former.

As the computer was booting up, she sat back in the chair and cradled the coffee in her hands. She was feeling shaky. It could have been sleep deprivation or, unfortunately, the lingering effects from the intensity of Kellen Falcon's stare.

Gabriel had informed the team about the surviving vampire, that he was an American and a former crime scene investigator from Necropolis. An expert in explosives. A rather convenient fact, she thought, considering the circumstances. And likely the reason he was at the top of Gabriel's suspect list.

She didn't usually think the worst of people, but she'd been a crime scene investigator long enough to know that everyone had a darkness inside them. It just took the right environment and perfect circumstances to bring it out. Maybe these had been Kellen's.

She certainly knew the unpredictability of vampires. Male ones in particular. Jean-Paul had schooled her in that regard quite effectively.

It had been over two years since her torrid affair with the flamboyant three-hundred-year-old vampire, but the bad taste still lingered in her mouth. So much that just being around another male vampire sent an involuntary shudder down her spine.

It didn't help matters that her father, also her pack's alpha, continually reminded her of those two months of rebellion. Usually, he was trying to make a point about her un-lycan behavior by reminding her how disappointed he'd been in her, how embarrassing it had been for him, as head of the pack, how she couldn't possibly give him a bunch of grandkids with a being who couldn't produce children. And God forbid, if her pups ended up inbred.

"No alpha daughter of mine should be prancing around with a bloodsucker. It's beneath all that the pack stands for." His words battered at her mind at the most inconvenient times. Like now, when the power of Kellen's gaze still lingered on her skin.

Setting her cup down, she rubbed her hands down her arms, trying to scrub away the gooseflesh that had popped up all over. She scolded herself for reacting this way. It wasn't as if the vampire was all that good-looking. He wasn't drop-dead gorgeous, as Jean-Paul had been, with his long, black hair and alabaster skin.

No, Kellen had been almost average-looking, more than average—tall, long legs, very short, dark-brown hair. He definitely had the perfect pale skin going, along with cut cheekbones and strong jaw, but it was his fierce eyes that rattled her. When he had looked at her, albeit briefly, she felt an instantaneous jolt. Like an arrow had pierced her, but without the insurmountable pain such an event would have caused.

She shivered again and tried to force his image from her mind. She hoped that this would be the last time she would see him; she really didn't need the problems that his presence could cause her. Her father had been on her back enough about settling down with a proper mate and having a litter of children. Pity the thought. That was the last thing in this life that she wanted. She had other things to do before she even considered kids.

But her father was insistent, even going so far as sending her dossiers on potential mates. In the past two months, he'd sent her five possible candidates. All lycans of course, except for one witch—the son of one of his old college buddies. He'd compiled information on everything, from their family backgrounds to their income to their favorite foods. She'd barely perused any of them, finding the situation completely absurd and irritating.

When she was ready to find a mate, she'd choose someone who made her laugh and gave her that belly-dropping feeling just by one look.

Another image of Kellen popped up in her head. Cursing, she shoved it away, then rolled her chair closer to the computer and got to work.

She plugged the information for the city of Nouveau Monde business pages into her search engine. Because the medical center was run and paid for by the city, all of the electrical, heating and phone services were also taken care of by the city.

After a quick search of the city's website, Sophie found the number for repairs. She picked up the phone and dialed. It was around one in the morning, but she knew someone would be there. That was the beauty of having night-stalking species working for all branches of the city government.

After a ten-minute conversation with an energetic employee named Berta, Sophie had a list of mechanical and electrical problems logged into the city's repair system over the past year. None of them had been heating-related. There hadn't been any complaints lodged about the center's boilers or any major electrical problems. Just small jobs, like a bank of fluorescent tubes blanking out on the second floor, or the phones going out in one of the smaller offices. Nothing glaring that pointed to a major issue that would blow up Dr. Bueller's medical offices.

Certainly, she'd dig more into the building. She already set up an electrical wiring inspection for later today, and she had someone coming in to look at the boilers. But as it stood, it was looking more and more like the explosion had been deliberate.

Sighing, she lifted her hands to her head and pulled off the elastic band holding up her hair. She ran her hands through her long, red hair and rubbed at the back of her head where the beginning of a headache was brewing. It was going to be an even longer morning than it had been a night—if that was possible.

Sophie's fellow investigator, Olena Petrovich, a vampiress from Russia, took that moment to glide into the room, looking just as fresh and spry as she did earlier in the evening. She didn't know how the vampiress did it, but for as long as she knew Olena, she never looked rumpled or tired. It was as if she thrived on all the activity.

"It's official. Our victims died from a big explosion." She slid onto the edge of Sophie's desk, coroner's report in hand.

"Anything else interesting?" Sophie asked.

"We're still missing three pieces of Dr. Bueller and one piece of the lycan victim."

"Anything else that won't make me lose my late-night sandwich and coffee?"

"All the vampire patients had *Sangcerritus.* And the lycan had something called *Immune-Medicated Hemolytic Anemia.*"

Sophie shrugged; she never heard of the disease. It was very rare for a lycan to contract any type of disease. But she supposed, if the lycan in question was unsanitary and didn't uphold any standards for what he ate, he could contract an illness usually reserved for canines.

"I guess the poor guy suffered from *pica,* as well, because of the anemia. The coroner found a bunch of concrete and dirt in the guy's stomach."

Sophie shook her head, unable to imagine what that infliction would be like. She was familiar with the vampire disease *Sangcerritus*, though. A close vampire girlfriend of hers contracted it years ago. It was one of those diseases like cancer. It could inflict any vampire, but it was rare—only one in a hundred thousand would contract it.

Unfortunately, her friend didn't survive. It wasn't exactly the disease that killed her—vampires could go for years before it finally shut down all their systems—but what it did to her mind…. She went mad and ended up taking her own life by jumping out of her twenty-first-story apartment window at sunny high noon.

Sophie had been first on the scene. It was a horrendous way to discover that one of your close friends was dead. Sometimes late at night, she could still see her friend's broken and bloody body and dead stare in her mind. Hazards of the job, she supposed.

She wondered if Kellen had the blood disorder, if that was why he'd been in Dr. Bueller's office. She pitied him, if that was the reason.

As if reading her mind, Olena said, "I wonder if tall, dark and handsome was there for the same illness."

"Who?" She played ignorant. She really didn't want Olena to know she'd just been thinking about him. The vampiress was relentless when it came to men, especially attractive men.

"Kellen Falcon, the surviving vampire from the medical center." She arched her perfectly manicured eyebrows. "I know you noticed him."

"No, I didn't."

Olena smiled. "Sophie, my dear, you're lying to a woman who has had centuries of sexual experience. I know when someone is interested and when they aren't."

"*Ne pas être sot.* I'm not interested in him. He's a suspect in a crime, Olena."

"So?" She wriggled her eyebrows. "It would make for a rather interesting tryst, *n'est ce pas?*"

Sophie crinkled her nose at that. "I'm not interested in trysts with anyone, especially vampires." She took a sip of her coffee. "If you recall, Jean-Paul was the worst thing that ever happened to me."

Olena waved her hand as if batting away a fly. "He was a fool and an idiot." She slid off the desk. "Kellen Falcon does not strike me as either of those things."

Sophie watched her leave just as elegantly as she had arrived, and cursed under her breath. Take it for Olena to plant the seeds of curiosity in her head. The woman was gifted in all things relating to love and sex. Especially the sex part.

Leaning back in her chair, she stared at the computer screen, trying to wrestle those seeds out of her mind. Because if they remained for long, they would take root and grow. And the last thing Sophie needed was another vampire in her life.

Chapter 4

Tick.

Tick.

Tick.

The incessant sound tapped at his head like a wood-pecker on a tree trunk.

Kellen sat in the corner of his room and watched the walls slowly starting to close in. Inch by inch they pressed down on him, making the room seem smaller, cramped, stifling. Heat from the register permeated the confining area, making it difficult to breathe.

The heat waves appeared to be melting the wallpaper off the walls. He wiped at his eyes trying to clear his vision. It didn't help much.

Every way Kellen moved, it felt as if his head was caving in. Even sticking his head out of the open window gave no relief to his growing claustrophobia. Lying down had just caused the bed to spin. And sitting on the sofa watching television made him feel like he was being sucked into the screen.

He was in bad shape and it was getting progressively worse.

If he didn't do something soon to focus on something else, Kellen was afraid of what he might do. The last thing he needed was to get kicked out of the city or get arrested for tearing apart his hotel room—even though that was exactly what he wanted to do. His fingers itched to destroy something. It was a bad place to be in without any help.

Kellen put on a fresh set of clothes, walked out from his hotel and hailed a taxi. Until he slid into the vehicle's backseat, he didn't have a real plan. The second he did, he told the driver to take him to the central police headquarters. Since he was in such a combative mood, he might as well find some people to bicker with.

The fiery woman with the ice-laced eyes seemed like the perfect sparring partner.

Twenty minutes later, Kellen stood in the lobby of the Nouveau Monde Otherworld Police Department, or NMOPD, trying to convince the witch receptionist to let him in. He was failing miserably and becoming more irritable with every passing minute. He needed to be doing something to help them solve the crime—

why the medical center exploded. It was right up his alley.

"If you don't have an official visitor's pass, I can't let you in," she informed him again, as she tapped her ball-point pen repeatedly on the top of the receptionist desk.

In a way, she reminded him of Lyra Magice, the witch he had worked with at the OCU. Aloof, yet feisty when pressed. He had liked that about Lyra. She had ended up marrying a dhampir, a wealthy half vamp, half witch from Nouveau Monde. She was happy, and Kellen had been happy for her, even if he had never told her.

"I could try Inspector Bellmonte's cell phone again for you, Monsieur Falcon."

"Thank you."

Stepping back from the counter to give her room to make the call, Kellen watched the bustling of the department as it ebbed and flowed. Uniformed officers and plainclothes personnel moved through the open, airy lobby with purpose and intent. Some chatted with others, but most walked alone, expressions of determination or contemplation on their faces. It made him homesick for the police headquarters in Necropolis, although this place looked nothing like the OCU.

With wide, tall windows and welcoming, high-arched ceilings, the NMOPD made a person feel wanted. The dark and cramped space in Necropolis always brought thoughts of depression and isolation. Again, the difference between the cities was evident even in the building design.

Or it could have been that Kellen was merely seeking a refuge—a place where he could finally feel at home. He didn't really know how long he had; his doctor had informed him that his disease was progressive, and it already was making its way to his brain, where it would eventually kill him. Most vampires went mad first, though. He was running out of time.

But the disease running rampant in his system was doing more than ticking down a clock. It was counting down his days of seeking a true happiness, one that maybe he wasn't meant to ever possess. He actually had never contemplated happiness until he'd been diagnosed. Knowing that death was knocking at the door made him sit up, take notice and then take stock of his life. So far, Kellen hadn't been too impressed with his stock.

He rubbed a hand over his head, trying to shove away the maudlin thoughts. Not one for introspection, Kellen's philosophy was usually to live life without regret. He hated that little needling doubts were starting to interfere with his outlook. If he was going to die soon from the disease making a home in his mind, then he'd go out with a bang.

The receptionist kept her eye on him as she dialed the inspector's number. He nodded to her and she smiled. A commotion drew Kellen's attention, as two uniforms struggled with a man in custody. The man was trying to wiggle his way out of the handcuffs and the hands gripping his arms. And doing a fine job of it,

Kellen thought. The officers had to shove him to the ground to reassert their control over him.

Everyone in the lobby was watching the spectacle. It was a perfect distraction for Kellen.

Looking around to make sure no one was watching him, he moved toward the double glass doors separating the main lobby from the crime lab. He straightened his shoulders and pushed through. He walked with his head up as if he belonged there. The first two people he went by didn't even make eye contact with him.

Every room he passed with an open door, Kellen peered in. Most were offices with important-looking people at large wooden desks. Some glanced up as he looked in, but most were too busy with whatever tasks they had been assigned to notice.

After turning several corners and walking three different hallways, he came across what looked like to be the official crime scene tech labs. He inhaled the familiar smell of disinfectant, bleach and other chemicals, and smiled. To him, it was as homey as apple pie.

A familiar, accented voice floated down the hall and it quickened his pace. As he neared a large-windowed room, he noticed both crime scene techs from the medical center bent over, inspecting what looked like a lot of burnt debris spread out over an eight-square-foot plastic and metal table. He stopped and leaned against the wall, enjoying the view for a moment.

The vampiress had a striking figure, showcased amply in black slacks and a teal-colored blouse. Her sable hair flowed around her chiseled features, making her cheekbones stand out even more, as well as her intense green eyes. She possessed that regal beauty that queens and princesses displayed after years of being worshipped. It wouldn't surprise him that she had a long line of adoring men at her beck and call.

Despite all that, it was the lycan who stole his gaze and occupied his mind.

The lycan's hair was still up in a high ponytail, and it swung back and forth as she moved her head. He could just imagine what all that glorious, shiny red hair would look like cascading around her shoulders and down her back—her naked back.

Her face was scrubbed clean of any makeup. A smattering of freckles dotted the bridge of her nose. Her blue eyes were luminous and deep-set, and she had a wide, full mouth, unpainted and perfect. He'd been thinking about those lips for hours now.

It must have been because she seemed so prickly that he'd been thinking about her. Kellen loved a challenge in any form.

It didn't take long before the lycan sensed his probing stare.

Stiffening, she glanced over her shoulder and met his gaze. The punch in his gut was instantaneous. The woman was intense. He didn't usually like reserved, aloof women, preferring those that were up for some fun. No one too complicated. The redhead had "complications" written all over her.

The vampiress also looked in his direction, but her gaze was anything but hostile. She smiled, which Kellen believed just spurred the lycan's hostility even more. He didn't need to know how to speak French—although he did—to understand the slew of curses she grunted. Those types of expletives were universal.

The vampiress leaned out of the open doorway. "Are you lost?"

He smiled. "Do I look lost?"

"Maybe a little." She returned his smile, her fangs peeking out between ruby-red lips.

Pushing off the wall, he held out his hand. "Kellen Falcon."

"Olena Petrovich." She took his hand and shook it, pulling him over the threshold. Tingles of power radiated up his arm like electricity. Those prickles were pleasant on his skin. He'd gone too long without bonding with another vampire. "I know who you are. Gabriel told us to watch out for you."

"Now, why would he say that?"

"Oh, I'm sure there are plenty of reasons why," she purred.

The lycan rolled her eyes. "Oh, for the moon's sake, Olena, quit flirting with him."

Olena waved her hand in the lycan's direction. "Oh, and this is Sophie St. Clair."

Kellen glanced past Olena to the fiery lycan. Her gaze was penetrating.

"You shouldn't be in the lab. You don't have any authorization." She dug a cell phone from her pants pocket and flipped it open. "I'm calling security."

Olena released her hold on his hand and shook her head. "Oh, Sophie, don't be rude."

"He's interfering with an investigation." She lifted her phone when Olena tried to make a grab for it. "He's a suspect, Olena."

"Not anymore he's not," declared the inspector as he came around the corner and into view. On an angry sigh, Sophie snapped her phone closed and slid it back into her pocket. Kellen had the pleasure of seeing her eyes flash angrily in his direction. Gabriel continued. "I talked to Caine and he vouches that you are not a crazy person who we should be worried about."

"Oh, good," Kellen mocked, his hand over his heart. "I was starting to have doubts myself."

"He still shouldn't be here, Gabe. This is an investigation and no place for a civilian, especially a victim of the explosion."

Smiling at her, Kellen made certain she knew he was doing a slow perusal of her body. She was a tight little package: pert breasts, small waist, curvy hips. Lean, lithe, and he imagined, given her species, extremely agile. When his gaze landed finally on her face, her eyes seemed to almost ice over, and he swore he could see puffs of condensed steam coming from her nose.

"Well, since I'm already here, and *not* a civilian, I could help out." As he danced around the lycan, he swore he could feel her jaws snapping at the back of his neck. He made his way to the table and pointed to a tiny piece of copper wire. "Because, as I see it, your unexplained explosion just turned into a bomb."

Chapter 5

Sophie stomped to the table and stared down at where Kellen pointed. "A piece of wire could mean anything. You're jumping to conclusions."

He pointed to something else on the table. "That's definitely a piece of aluminum casing from a cell phone." He moved his finger over another part of the table. "And those are steel ball bearings. Put all those things together and you get an improvised explosive device, or IED for short."

She hated that the vampire appeared to be correct. She knew she would have seen it eventually, given the opportunity to look and investigate. Explosives weren't part of her expertise, but it irked her that he had seen those things in a matter of seconds of scanning the surface of the table. She'd been looking at this stuff for an hour already.

"Olena, get our new special investigative consultant a pair of latex gloves," Gabriel said. "I'll get you a crime scene visitor's pass from the front desk, so you can just walk in next time and not have to sneak by."

Kellen nodded, but glanced pointedly at Sophie. "That would be great, Inspector."

Swiveling around, she glared at the inspector. "Gabe, a word outside, please?"

He stepped out and she followed him, shutting the door firmly behind her. She was talking even before he had a chance to turn around and face her. "This is a big mistake, and you know it."

"Kellen has extensive knowledge of explosives. He worked in the crime lab in Necropolis. He will be an asset."

"He was a suspect just half an hour ago."

"But he isn't now. Besides, we've been short-staffed and lacking an expert in explosives. If he can help us out in that regard, I'm taking advantage of it."

Sophie crossed her arms, trying to think of another argument. Unfortunately, she couldn't think of another logical one, except that Kellen Falcon made her nervous. But she didn't want to confess that to Gabriel.

"It's not because he's a vampire, is it?"

"No, of course not. I'm offended you would ask me something like that."

Gabriel eyed her, probably remembering all the problems she had with Jean-Paul—all the drama she had inadvertently brought to work because of him— then smiled, patting her on the shoulder. "Good. Now, I expect you to afford all the courtesy you can muster to Kellen. You don't have to like him—I'm not quite sure that I do—but you have to work with him." Looking past her shoulder, he shook his head. "At least Olena won't have a problem."

Sophie turned around to see Olena with her hand on Kellen's muscular arm, a saucy smile on her lips, and a twinkle in her radiant green eyes. The vampiress was a born flirt. She possessed the power of seduction, but Sophie knew she hardly used it. She didn't need to. Olena was drop-dead gorgeous, with an ego almost as big as her bust.

As she watched Kellen return Olena's smile and respond to her flirtatious touch, the hair on the back of her neck stirred to attention. Feeling strange, she rubbed her hand under her ponytail, trying to chase away the sensation. Her body was responding as if she were jealous, which was absolutely ridiculous.

"I'm out of here," Gabriel said, jostling Sophie from her reverie. "I have to return to the crime scene."

"Okay. We'll get started on this mess."

"I'll need a report in four hours for the superinten-dent."

She nodded, knowing full well the superintendent would be breathing down Gabriel's neck for an answer. He'd have to alert the media soon, as to what was going on. Reporters were already hovering in front of the headquarters, waiting for any kind of sound bite.

"Oh, by the way, Duncan is looking for you." With that little gem of information, Gabriel tipped his hat with his finger and made his exit.

Groaning, Sophie wrapped her hand around the doorknob to open the door, but she wasn't quick enough to escape. Duncan Quinn, six feet and two hundred pounds of Irish lycan, came striding around the corner.

"Sophie. Hey. How are you?"

She rolled her eyes at his attempt to appear surprised that he had run into her, when she knew he'd been looking for her, as he had almost every day for the past month at about this time. He'd been like a lost little puppy, drooling after her ever since she agreed to go out on one date with him. He'd been one of the five suitable suitors her father had handpicked for her. She'd agreed to a date, just to get her father off her back.

Duncan had taken her to dinner. It was pleasant enough. He talked to her, asked her the appropriate questions, held out her chair and poured her wine, but ultimately it had been one of the more boring evenings she'd spent with a man. It had been like going out with a friend, and not a very good friend at that. Duncan was a nice guy, but dull as drywall dust.

Her father's words sounded in her head: "Twenty-eight is too old for a lycan female to not be married and raising children." He claimed that Duncan would be a good match for her.

"Hi, Duncan."

"How's your day been?"

"Not bad, considering I've been forced to work with a civilian."

Duncan followed her line of sight. His brow went up at the sight of Kellen and Olena laughing. "Who's the guy?"

"He's an American from Necropolis. I guess he worked for their crime lab there."

"What's he doing here in Nouveau Monde?"

"I'm not sure. He was at the medical center when the explosion occurred."

Duncan sniffed. "Maybe he was the one that blew it up."

"He's not a suspect." Crossing her arms, she glared at him. "And who gave you the authority to make wild accusations like that?"

He seemed to shrink a little at her harsh words. No small feat, considering Duncan's size. He put his hand up in defense. "Hey, I'm just making a joke, Sophie. Relax."

"Well, it's not funny." Sophie looked past Duncan and met Kellen's gaze. He was staring at her through the glass, with a look of hard contemplation on his face. Had he heard their conversation? She knew some vampires had superior hearing. Not as superior as lycans, but certainly more than any average human.

The way he regarded her made her quiver. Her thighs clenched tight, and she shifted her stance, uncomfortable with the tingling sensations radiating over her skin. His sky-blue eyes were intense. Powerful. And strangely possessive.

Sophie put her hand on the door handle again, turning it open. "I've got to get back to work, Duncan."

She really didn't want to enter the room, not with the way Kellen was making her feel, unnerved and confused, but she wanted to escape Duncan's persistent courting even more. The lesser of two evils, she supposed.

Duncan stopped her with a hand on her arm. "Can I take you to dinner Friday night?"

"I don't know, Duncan. I imagine this case will be taking up most of my time in the next few days."

"Yeah, but you can't work twenty-four hours a day every day. You have to take time out eventually, and you have to eat."

She nodded, not meeting his gaze. "I know. I'll call you, okay?"

"Sure." He tucked his hand into his jeans pocket.

As she pushed open the door and walked into the room, Sophie was fully aware of Duncan's gaze on her back, and Kellen's on her front. Trying to maintain her composure, she shut the door firmly behind her and moved to the table.

"What did the mighty Irishman want?" Olena asked.

"The usual." Sophie snapped on some new latex gloves and took up a spot alongside the table. "Dinner."

"Your boyfriend didn't look too happy," Kellen said, as he took up a place on the opposite side of the table from Sophie.

"He's not my boyfriend, if it's any of your business. Which it's not."

"Definitely, not from a lack of trying," Olena offered, as she picked her way through the debris on the table, sorting similar material into one of the five plastic bins sitting along the side.

Sophie ignored her response and dipped her head to examine a piece of metal that looked like a screw. She didn't want to discuss it, especially not with Kellen present. For some reason, the last thing she wanted to discuss in front of him was her love life or lack there of.

"I am so happy I'm not a lycan," Olena mused. "To be pressured into mating with someone you don't even particularly like." She smiled. "Being a vampire is so much more liberating, isn't it, Kellen?"

Sophie lifted her gaze to Kellen. He was watching her out of the side of his eyes as he smiled at Olena. He had an electric smile, the white of his fangs peeking out from between full, sensuous lips. Even from here, she could sense its power.

"Yes. I'd rather mate with whomever I please."

Olena nodded. "Me, too."

Sophie tossed a piece of melted plastic into another of the bins. "Okay, let's just shut up and get to work."

Before she could lower her gaze, she caught Kellen looking at her. One side of his wide mouth was tilted up. He looked like a man who knew a secret.

Her secret.

Chapter 6

After about three hours of picking through the debris the crime scene team had collected, Kellen, Sophie and Olena managed to fill all five plastic bins with various materials. The metal bin was the fullest. As Kellen laid out various steel fragments, wire, ball bearings and a steel cap, his suspicions were confirmed about a bomb being the cause of the explosion.

"It appears to be a pipe bomb," Kellen explained to Gabriel and Superintendent Jakob Weiss, as he and the crime scene team, consisting of Olena, Sophie and a young witch named François, who Kellen kept calling Frank, sat around a table in a private board room. His new special consultant badge was hanging around his neck, since he was wearing a T-shirt and had no pocket to clip it to.

"Do we know what kind of casing it was in?" Gabriel asked.

Kellen opened his mouth to respond, but Sophie beat him to it. "By the amount of black leather fragments and vinyl parts, it was probably inside a black leather briefcase."

The superintendent, a tall, spindly vampire, who Kellen thought resembled Bela Lugosi himself, worried a weathered hand through his salt-and-pepper hair. "Are you saying this is another terrorist attack?"

Flinching, Kellen stared at Gabriel, eyebrow raised. "*Another* terrorist attack? Am I missing something here?"

"A few months ago there was an explosion in one of the blood bars downtown. A group calling themselves NORM, Non-Otherworlder Resistance Movement, claimed responsibility for it."

"NORM. That's original," Kellen smirked. "Any causalities?"

He shook his head. "Thankfully, the bomb went off during the day."

"Purposely or accidentally?" Kellen asked. Sometimes bombs misfired, going off when they weren't supposed to. If this one was set to go off during a time when no one was inside, it would help explain the intent of the group—to intimidate, or to terminate.

"Why does it matter?" Jakob asked.

"It shows motivation. For revenge, to make a point, to terrorize, to kill. A bomber bombs for a reason."

"We believe it was purposely set for daytime," Gabriel answered.

"Did they use a pipe bomb?"

The inspector shook his head.

"Do you think this group wants to kill a bunch of Otherworlders?"

The superintendent responded, "All terrorists are the same, and they need to be stopped." He shook Gabriel's hand. "Thank you, Inspector, for your hard work. I'll take all of this into account when I hold my press conference at nine. Make sure we are following *all* leads. I'll inform the human authorities, so we can coordinate a task force to investigate this NORM group."

"I'll keep you apprised of any developments in the investigation, Superintendent."

With the barest of nods to the rest of the team, the superintendent left the room, his two aides in three-piece suits following him out.

Gabriel sat on the edge of the large table. "The pressure is on to solve this one. We have probably twelve hours before there's a panic in the city, especially if the superintendent spins the terrorist angle."

"Which we know he will," Olena added.

"Sophie, you're working with Kellen to put the bomb and casing together. I want an exact replica to work with."

Amused, Kellen watched as Sophie bristled in her chair, but she kept her mouth closed, which was curious. He fully expected her to protest working with him. Maybe it was the way the inspector looked at her while he talked that made her hold her tongue. The lycan could be intimidating when he wanted to, without any effort at all. Maybe because they were both lycans who belonged to the same pack—and this was some pack of politics at play. Whatever it was, he enjoyed seeing her squirm.

"Olena and I will work on the victims and see what we can find there. François, I want you to go through the surveillance footage of that day and look for anyone coming to the ninth floor with a black briefcase."

The kid stopped chewing the end of his pencil and said, "It's an office building. Do you know how many people have briefcases?"

Gabriel smiled. "No, but you will after today. I want screen shots with time stamps of every single one."

François groaned, then went back to chewing on his pencil.

Gabriel stood, signaling the end of the meeting. "To work. I'd like to get some headway before the end of the shift."

Everyone else filed out of the room. Kellen trailed behind Sophie, hyperaware of the anger coursing through her. It was almost like sitting near a campfire. Hot. Almost too hot, but Kellen had always liked the heat.

She didn't say a word as they returned to the examining room to reconstruct the bomb and briefcase. She snapped on a pair of gloves and got to work on the bin of plastics and leather, taking out one piece at a time and lining it up on her half of the worktable. The other half was reserved for him to put together the pipe bomb.

"You don't look too happy about something," he commented, as he put on his gloves.

Without looking up at him, she said, "I am in charge here, *d'accord*? You do what I tell you to do. You are my helper. You understand that?"

"Yup. Perfectly." Her anger amused him. Not that she didn't have a right to her anger. She certainly did. He understood it. But he sensed that the anger was also mixed with another emotion—desire. He wondered if that was angering her the most.

As Kellen quickly put together what was shaping up to be two pieces of metal water pipes, strapped together to form the IED, he watched Sophie work. He couldn't help it. The way she moved, so fluid and lithe, sparked a fresh bout of desire in his gut. He particularly enjoyed the way she worried her full bottom lip while she figured something out.

The incessant ticking of his inner clock seemed to slow somewhat as he watched her. Her presence calmed him in a way nothing else had managed to accomplish.

With an angry sigh, she slammed her hand down on the table and jerked her head up to glare at him. "Would you quit watching me," she bit out between gritted teeth.

"I can't help myself. I like the view."

She frowned. "You're distracting me."

He grinned at that. "Am I now?"

Shaking her head, she focused back on her work. *"L'homme est fou."*

"I'm not that crazy." He smiled. "I understand French. I was born and raised in New Orleans. My mother…now, she was the crazy one." He rolled his eyes.

Sophie smiled, but she lowered her head to try to hide it.

"I like your smile. You should do it more often."

Her smile broadened. *"Merci."*

"De rien."

He laid out the final pieces of copper wiring that was part of the ignition, but what he really wanted to do was touch Sophie's skin. It looked like cream, and he imagined it would be as silky and soft as it appeared.

Trying to clamp down on the rising desire he was feeling, he cleared his suddenly dry throat and fiddled with the steel cap on the metal pipe. He lifted his head and stole another glance at Sophie. She was impossible *not* to look at. How could any man ignore such a magnificent creature? He swallowed again, realizing how corny he was beginning to sound.

Desire was desire to Kellen. It usually didn't ignite songs or poems in his mind—about a woman's beauty, or purple prose about lovemaking. If a woman was attractive, he craved her. If he had a chance to bed her, all the sweeter. It was as simple as that. Again, he didn't think simple and Sophie went together all that well.

"You must have the wolves lined up to date you." He winced at hearing the corniness of his words. It had sounded better in his mind. His usual confidence was waning, being alone with her.

Without looking up, she said, "Not really."

"Must be something wrong with them."

She looked at him then, her brow furrowed. "I am not so spectacular, not when a woman like Olena is in the room."

He heard a hitch in her words. Was she actually jealous of the vampiress? Sure, Olena was gorgeous and confident, but she was nothing, compared to Sophie. She had beauty that transcended physical traits.

Kellen couldn't put into words what he saw when he looked at her. The only thing he could compare it to was the awe he felt when seeing the first signs of dawn creeping through the Sistine Chapel and alighting on Michelangelo's masterpiece.

He couldn't tell her that, though. It sounded European-poet-creepy, even in his mind.

"Olena is nice to look at, sure." He swallowed, suddenly feeling apprehensive. "But you—you are…" he shook his head, trying to come up with words, any word that could do her justice, "…just, I don't know, more than that."

He cringed, thinking how stupid he must have

sounded, but he must have said something right, because a flush started at her neck and rushed up her face to stain her alabaster cheeks. The color brought out the peppering of freckles on the bridge of her nose and on her cheekbones.

She dipped her head to hide it. But he caught it. He also caught the flare of her nostrils. His scent, spurred by desire, must have been heavy in the air. He liked that she was inhaling it—maybe giving him some consideration.

"Listen," she began, "I appreciate your attraction to me. You are being incredibly flattering, but you know that it's pointless."

"Is it?"

She looked up and met his gaze. "Yes. For many reasons that I am sure you are aware of. First, because we are working together."

"And because of the big guy who was here earlier?"

She nodded. "Yes."

"I thought he wasn't your boyfriend."

"He's not."

Finally it hit him. He'd been blind to it for some reason—or didn't want to consider it. "Ah, I get it. Lycan." He pointed at her. "Vampire." He pointed at himself.

She nodded again. But he saw something flash in her eyes. Something akin to regret.

"Okay. That's cool. I was just worried it was because you didn't find me irresistible, which I know now isn't the reason."

She shook her head, but there was a small smile on her lips. "Is it because you are American that you speak so brashly?"

"Nah. It's because I have no sense. I just say what's on my mind." He shrugged. "It's a gift."

"From your crazy mother?" She smiled, then started to laugh.

He joined in. "Yes, from her."

Chapter 7

Sophie and Kellen worked in silence for the next two hours. And to Sophie's surprise, it was a comfortable time—one that usually came after years of knowing a colleague and working together. Nerves still wracked her body, though now for completely different reasons.

The man was an enigma. One she wasn't certain she wanted to figure out or had any business figuring out. Like she had told him—she was lycan, he was vampire. Not a very stable mix.

After hours of work they had managed to put together replicas of both the casing and the bomb.

The casing was what she had suspected—an ordinary black leather briefcase with a structured box lining and leather-wrapped handle, an item that could be bought at any luggage or office store.

The bomb on the other hand, according to Kellen, wasn't so run-of-the-mill.

"This is old-school stuff." He ran his gloved finger over the three metal pipes banded together by leather straps.

She watched as his fingers seem to stroke the mechanism, and she wondered what his fingers would feel like on her skin. But she had no business thinking about Kellen like that, because he wasn't lycan. Her attraction to him made her uneasy. Her pack alpha would chastise her for feeling this way. But she couldn't seem to help it.

Shaking the carnal thoughts from her mind, she turned her attention back onto the bomb. "What kind of trigger was used, do you think?"

He pointed to a piece of plastic with two numbers on it sitting on the table. "I was wrong about the cell phone. Too sophisticated. They used some kind of timing mechanism." He picked up the plastic piece and scraped at the black charring to reveal a white background. "An egg timer, I bet. They're easy to find and easy to use. Untraceable."

"How do you know so much about bombs?"

"I used to make them in the war." He picked up the reassembled bomb and examined it intently.

"Which war?"

"World War Two and Vietnam."

She eyed him intently. "A regular war hero."

He shrugged. "Nah, not a hero. I just like to blow stuff up."

"I can picture you as a soldier."

He nodded and put the bomb down on the table. "I looked pretty good in a uniform, too."

Sophie smiled. She could picture him in a uniform. He had the type of sublime male physique that could fill one out perfectly. Wide shoulders, trim waist, long legs. He had the powerful form of someone who could run a mile without any effort, or lift a man off his feet with one hand. When he moved, she could see the way the muscles rippled and bunched.

Pulling herself from her fantasy, she lowered her gaze before Kellen noticed that she was checking him out.

But it was too late; he was grinning at her as if he knew every detail in her mind. She hoped he wasn't one of those vampires that possessed that type of power. It would be way too uncomfortable if he could read every notion in her head. In the future, she'd have to control her thoughts and steer them away from wondering what he looked like naked.

"I still have the uniform. I could put it on for you sometime." He cocked an eyebrow seductively.

Looking around her, Sophie noticed that she had moved closer to Kellen. There was now only a foot of space between them, and she could feel the heat of his body and hear the steady rhythm of his heart. Flaring her nostrils, she inhaled his scent. Everyone possessed a certain smell. Lycans and witches smelled earthy, vampires always smelled like spices. Kellen's scent was strong and tasty, like cinnamon.

A sudden urge to touch him surged over her. Unable to resist it, she lifted her hand and breached the distance between them. But before she could lay her finger on him, Olena burst through the door in a cloud of expensive designer perfume, chattering like a songbird.

Sophie retreated a few steps as the vampiress swooped over them.

"Who is hungry?" Olena wrapped her hand around Kellen's arm as was her habit when she talked to people. Actually, when she talked to *men*. "I know a great place for breakfast."

"I could eat," he answered, but he had yet to take his eyes off Sophie. Her skin was tingling as if a phantom energy was caressing her. Was he doing that to her?

She could feel her face start to redden. Turning to hide her blush, she moved around the table and stood by her briefcase model. "I'll pass, thank you, Olena. I think I'm going to do some more work and see if François has printed out any photos to compare this to."

Olena waved her hand at Sophie. "You work too much. I always tell you to relax, but you never listen." She snuggled up to Kellen. "I guess it is just you and me, handsome."

"I guess so." He turned his attention to Olena and forced a smile—but it didn't quite reach his eyes.

Sophie tried not to watch as Kellen and Olena walked out of the room, arm in arm, chatting like old friends.

Jealousy knifed her in the stomach, cutting her to the bone.

Logically, she knew she shouldn't be jealous. She was a lycan, a loyal pack member with a long list of lycan suitors who would fight tooth and nail for a chance to court her. But at this moment she didn't find any one of them very agreeable.

If she went down the list, she could find something wrong with each and every one of them. In Duncan's case, he was too boring, and not all that intelligent. His idea of great literature was the *Sports Illustrated* swimsuit edition, which bothered her twofold, because Sophie never considered herself to be swimsuit model material. She wasn't voluptuous. More athletic than bodacious. She never understood what Duncan possibly saw in her. Judging from his past conquests, she definitely wasn't his type—voluptuous, with more boobs than brains. Maybe the alpha was forcing him into it, just as he was pushing her, which wouldn't surprise her. A pairing between her and Duncan would be a political coup. Her father and Duncan's father went way back.

Sometimes she hated pack rules and politics. It would be nice to have the freedom to pick whatever mate she wanted. Born and bred under pack law, Sophie knew what was expected from her. From a young age, she'd been told that one day she would claim a partner and a mate from the eligible lycan males in the pack. She would wed and make little lycans to populate the pack. Procreation was really important in the pack mandate, as was breeding with one's own kind to produce strong healthy pups.

Already, most of her childhood friends were married and had two or three children. She shuddered at the idea of being a stay-at-home mom raising pups. She had too much adventure in her to give it up right now. Maybe if she met the right man she'd feel differently. A man with confidence, intelligence and a wicked sense of humor.

Someone a lot like Kellen.

Not that she was thinking about mating with Kellen. He was attractive and all, but definitely not the type of man a woman settled down with. No, he was more the type for a fling, a rebellious and decadent affair.

Shaking her head, she shoved the thoughts of Kellen out of her mind and got back to thinking about the case. She left the workroom and headed down the hall to the video room, where François worked. She'd get a head start on trying to identify the briefcase in the surveillance photos.

When she reached the room, she peered in and saw François at his array of computer screens, flipping through multiple images at once.

She cleared her throat. "François, I was—"

Without looking up, he put up his hand, palm out toward her. *"Attend. Attend. Une minute."*

She had the urge to bite his head off, but because of his brilliance with computers and other things, she bit down on her tongue instead. He had lots of idiosyncrasies, his blunt way of dealing with people was just one of the many characteristics that made François who he was, however annoying he might be on most occasions.

He swiveled in his chair and frowned at her. "What do you want?"

"Photo printouts of any and all people entering the medical center with a briefcase in their hand."

He swiveled back to his desk, grabbed a huge stack of paper and swiveled around again. "Here you go. Three hundred and twenty-two of them." He shuffled his rolling chair toward her and plunked the heavy stack into her outstretched hands. "Enjoy."

She hefted the stack. "Are you kidding me?"

"Nope." With that, he pushed backward with his feet and went rolling back to his desk and started typing on his keyboard without another word.

Sighing, she glanced down at the stack and shook her head. She was in for a long day. She should have left for a break when she had a chance.

"Want some help?" Kellen spoke to her from behind.

She was startled, almost dropping the photos. He reached for her and covered his hands over hers, steadying the stack. Instantly, heat flashed up her arms and over her shoulders.

"I thought you went for breakfast."

"I wasn't hungry for…pancakes." He eyed her intensely.

A tingling sensation warmed her belly and she

couldn't stop the grin that blossomed on her face. It actually felt good to see him again, even if he'd only been gone a half hour at the most.

Stepping back, she pulled her hands out from his. She had to get a hold of herself. She was acting like a love-struck youngster, still in her teenage awkwardness. He was just a man, after all, nothing special, even with his sparkling blue eyes, killer grin that could melt ice from a hundred yards, and incredible body.

It didn't matter that when he gave her that devilish look her stomach flipped over in a loop de loop. He was a coworker, if only until they solved this case, and a vampire. He was hands-off. She would just have to remind herself again and again, especially when his scent ignited a flash fire between her thighs.

"Do you want to help me go through these?" she asked.

He shook his head. "No, not really."

Frowning, she cocked her hip. "Then what are you doing here?"

He took the stack of photos from her hands. "I thought we could get out of here and go do something else."

"Like what?" Nerves were zinging through her again. She couldn't believe she was considering leaving the lab with this man.

"Going back to the crime scene and analyzing the blast pattern. I have a theory that I want to check out."

Sophie released the breath she didn't realize she was holding, and laughed. She couldn't help it; it just burst out of her. She thought he was going to proposition her. The crazy thing was, she had been prepared to accept.

"Why are you laughing?" he asked, a twinkle in his eye, as if privy to her thoughts.

"I just thought…"

He smiled. "Why, Sophie St. Clair, what did you think I was going to ask you to do with me?"

She blushed. "Nothing."

He raised his arm, gesturing down the hall. "Maybe, after we check out the crime scene, we can do that particular nothing you had in mind."

Speechless, she walked alongside him to the exit. Confusion swirled in her head. The vampire exuded a lot of charm. But it was more than that. She'd had charming before with Jean-Paul. It was the way Kellen looked at her, like he had every right in the world to be flirting with her. As though he was entitled. He knew she was attracted to him, and he was capitalizing on it.

What bothered her the most though, was that she liked it. A lot.

Chapter 8

Kellen surveyed the blast pattern of the explosion. Several yellow markers indicating where certain debris had landed dotted the floor in a circular array. The center of the range pointed toward one of the doctor's examining rooms.

He stood in front of the blown out wall. "I wonder who the next patient was for this room."

Sophie stood beside him and flipped through her notebook. "According to the report from the receptionist and the schedule, you were."

"Hmm, good thing I was on the phone in the lobby." He walked through the ravaged doorway and into the examining room. Sophie followed him. Pointing to the scorched crater in the once green tile, he said, "That's where the briefcase would've been set. Someone just walked in and put it there. Maybe a patient?"

"Gabe is looking through patient records and the schedule for the day."

Kellen eyed the damage in the room and the proximity of where the bomb would have been stashed. Anyone could have walked into this room: the receptionist, the nurses, patients, and of course the doctor. What did they all have in common? Besides that they were all in the medical center, nothing obvious. The receptionist was human, the patients mostly vampires and one lycan, and the doctor was a vampire.

If it was an attack on Otherworlders, the group didn't factor in that humans also worked in the building. Kellen knew that terrorists were known to sacrifice their own for the good of the cause. He'd seen it before. But maybe the receptionist was in on it. Except, she had appeared way too calm to be close to a bomb about to go off. If she had been afraid, Kellen would have noticed it—as would anyone among the vampires or the lycan in the waiting room.

"Did you work the bombing at the blood bar?" he asked Sophie.

"Yes."

"Does it appear to be the same MO? Did they use a pipe bomb?"

She frowned and glanced around the room as if taking everything in for the first time. "They used plastique and a cell phone detonator."

"Then why go back to a simple pipe bomb? They would've done more damage with C-4."

"You don't think this was an attack from a terrorist group?"

He shook his head. "No, this was more localized. Whoever put this bomb here wanted to hurt someone in this office."

She eyed him intently. "Do you have any enemies?"

"Yeah, lots, but none who knew I was coming here." He shrugged.

"I'm being serious."

The way the bridge of her nose wrinkled when she frowned at him made him want to smooth it away with the stroke of his thumb. Instead, he shoved his hands in his jeans pockets, where they wouldn't get into too much trouble.

"So am I." He wandered out of the damaged room and back into the patient waiting area. Sophie trailed behind him.

Out of the corner of his eye he saw her scowl. Damn if he didn't love it when she scowled. It was sexy as hell. He wondered if she did everything with such fierce determination. Once more his thoughts ventured into the carnal realm. He imagined Sophie pressed against a wall, her eyes flashing, claws digging into his back as he pounded into her again and again.

The image was so intense it made him almost stagger back. His heart raced like wildfire and his thigh muscles clenched in anticipation. Her scent came to him on a wisp of air. He inhaled it deeply, implanting it in his mind and gut. He'd recognize it now for the rest of his days.

A touch on his arm brought him around, fangs bared. Sophie's eyes widened and she took a step backward, wariness furrowing her brow.

"What's wrong? Your eyes are glowing."

Taking in a deep breath, Kellen rubbed a hand over his face, trying desperately to wipe away the erotic images from his mind. It would do neither of them any good if he was constantly thinking about having sex with her. He couldn't function with those powerful images in his head. He had to do something about them. But the only thing he could think of was purging them by acting them out. Somehow, he didn't think Sophie would go for that, especially not for the sake of his peace of mind.

Despite the attraction he knew she felt, she had made it perfectly clear that nothing could or would happen between them. They were of different species, and her lycan sensibilities were too ingrained for her to step out of the pack's protocols.

It was too bad really, because he knew without a doubt that sex with Sophie would be spectacular.

"There's nothing to see. Let's get out of here." He started for the exit, hoping that the cool morning air would jolt him out of his fantasy.

"Stop," she called after him.

He kept moving, afraid of what he would do if he didn't. The rush of blood in his veins pounded like a hammer in his head. He had to get outside before he did something stupid. It was more than just lust pumping through his body. He could feel the rage of the disease starting to rise. He'd been lucky, and only had suffered a few attacks since being diagnosed. But this one felt like all of those combined.

Sophie caught up to him as the elevator doors slid open and he walked in. She grabbed his arm. "Where are you going?"

"To Dr. Bueller's house. I have a feeling he's at the center of this. It was his office that the bomb was placed in."

"You don't even know where he lives, and you don't have a car."

"I'm sure I can find it. I'm a resourceful kind of guy." He shrugged and looked at the numbers lighting up as they descended to the ground floor. He kept concentrating on them, instead of on the way his body was shaking. The way his hands itched to touch Sophie, to caress her, to take her then and there without a care.

"I'm in charge here, remember? We'll go where I say."

He kept staring at the numbers, and bit out between clenched teeth, "Fine. Where are we going?"

She didn't speak right away, but Kellen could tell she was considering what he had just said. "The doctor doesn't live that far from here. I suppose we could go there and take a look around."

"Great idea, Sophie. Wish I thought of it."

She cocked her hip. "You don't have to be sarcastic."

"Sure I do. It's part of my charm." Sweat rolled down his temples. He wiped at it, trying hard not to look at her. Her close proximity was driving him mad. He could feel the heat from her body, the smell of her skin and hair and hear the thumping of her heart.

Thud.

Thud.

Thud.

Like a ticking time bomb in his head.

A dangerous mixture especially in such a small, closed-in area.

"Are you okay? You look flushed." She reached out to touch his arm.

Shrinking back to the far wall, Kellen bit down on his bottom lip to stem the rising fury in his body. "Don't touch me."

"What's wrong? Can I help you?"

He shook his head. "I just need to get outside."

"You are sick."

He looked at her then and saw the sympathy in her eyes. He hated it. He didn't want her sympathy, not from her, not now. A battle between rage and desire warred inside as he watched her regard him. In one thought, he had her pinned against the elevator wall, his cock plunging into her heat, screams of pleasure echoing in his ear. In another, she was on the ground, begging for her life, Kellen's fangs buried deep into her throat, rivulets of blood streaming down her chest.

Mercifully, the elevator dinged and the doors slid open. Kellen scrambled out and strode across the lobby and through the main doors, into the bright sunlight of the morning. He found a bench in the shade of a giant oak tree and slid onto it, hanging his head between his legs. Taking in deep breaths of air, he tried to regulate his heart and bury the rage back into his diseased bloodstream.

After a few minutes, Kellen could feel a change. His heart slowed. The urge to ruin something with his hands and teeth evaporated into the crisp breeze. He could breathe again without his lungs burning with anger.

Movement on his right brought his head up.

Sophie sat beside him, her hands set primly on her thighs.

He ran a hand over his head. "Well, that was awkward."

"Is it *Sangcerritus*?"

He sighed and leaned back into the bench. "Yeah. Do you know it?"

She nodded. "I had a friend who was diagnosed a couple years ago."

"Had?" That was the last thing he wanted to hear, not when he had come to Nouveau Monde looking for a cure.

She nodded.

"What happened?"

Sophie met his gaze, and he fell into the vividness of her eyes. "Do you really want to know?"

"Yeah, why not? I can pretend all I want, but I know this disease has an expiration date stamped on it."

"She jumped off her apartment balcony on a beautiful, hot summer day. She was twenty-one stories up." She glanced up into the sky. "She left a note saying the voices in her head were driving her mad."

He sighed again and put his arm along the bench behind her shoulders. The tips of her hair skimmed his hand. He liked the feel of it on his skin. She flinched but didn't move away from him. He moved over and touched her shoulder, cupping his hand around her arm.

Sighing, she leaned into him. "I'm sorry you have the disease," she said.

"Don't be. I figure, if I didn't have this rushing through my blood I would never have come to Nouveau Monde." He chuckled. "Just think, you would never have had the pleasure of meeting me."

Her lips twitched. "Yes, that would have been terrible."

"I'll say." He squeezed her shoulder, then stood. He held out his hand for her. She took it and he pulled her up. "Come on, let's go play doctor…err, I mean, let's go to the doctor's house and solve this case."

Laughing, she punched him playfully. He smiled and made a grab for her. She danced out of his way, still laughing. He loved the sound of her throaty laugh. It made him feel alive and free. Emotions he hadn't felt in a very long time…

Chapter 9

Dr. Bueller's home was an upscale condominium on the tenth floor of a high-rise about nine blocks from the medical center. As of yet, no crime scene investigator had visited the place, so they had to stop by the lab and gather the keys from Inspector Bellmonte.

Gabriel didn't appear keen on them going to the doctor's residence, but he didn't say anything verbally when Sophie had informed him of their plans to search the place. He just dropped the keys in Sophie's hand, gave Kellen a hard look, then turned his attention back to the computer files he was searching through.

"Is the good doctor married?" Kellen asked as he moved across the gleaming tile of the front foyer and into the sparsely decorated main living area of Dr. Bueller's home.

Sophie read from her notebook. "Not married. No kids. No next of kin recorded."

Kellen glanced around the room as he snapped on a pair of latex gloves. Everything looked bland and utilitarian. A simple gray sofa, wood coffee table and large, almost-empty bookcase were the only furniture in the living room. There were no paintings or pictures on the whitewashed walls to warm the room. No speck of dirt or dust coated the surfaces of the meager furnishings or the polished hardwood floor. If Kellen didn't know better, he'd assume that no one was living here.

He wandered into the kitchen to find the same emptiness. Pulling open the refrigerator door, he scanned the contents, finding almost nothing except a bottle of orange juice and some eggs. There weren't even any condiments lining the shelves. He opened the freezer, finding it full of single-serving frozen dinners. Most vampires enjoyed a healthy appetite for all of life's extravagances, food being one of them. Obviously, the good doctor didn't fall into that category.

"Wow, that's even more pathetic than my refrigerator," Sophie said from behind him, as she set her stainless steel crime scene collecting kit onto the center island.

After closing the freezer door, Kellen started opening and shutting counter drawers. "It doesn't even seem like he was living here."

Sophie pulled open some cupboard doors only to

find them empty. "Maybe he spent his time at a girl-friend's...or boyfriend's, for that matter."

"Maybe." He scanned the kitchen one last time, then moved down the hall. "I'm going to check the bedroom."

"I'll check the bathroom," Sophie called back.

Kellen liked that the two of them had already established a groove in working together. Sophie had made it known that she was in charge, but she had yet to shove it down his throat. He had stepped into the job as if he'd been working with her for years. It was a comfortable rhythm they were in, and more than that, he enjoyed being around her.

The bedroom was huge, appearing even more so because of the lack of furniture. Only two things took up space in the room: a neatly made bed and an old wooden desk, pushed up against the far wall near the bay window. There were no dresser drawers or night tables. Marching to the closet doors, Kellen wrenched them open and found a few dress shirts and suits hanging. Two pairs of dress shoes sat below on the carpeted floor.

On hands and knees, Kellen searched under the bed and found nothing—no dirty clothes, no neglected pair of slippers, not even any dust bunnies. Standing, he walked to the desk, then sat down in the rolling, ergonomic chair, systematically pulling open the drawers. The three along the side opened with no problem. Inside one was a ream of blank white paper. Another held a three-hole punch and an empty three-ring binder. The third, smaller drawer was full of pens and pencils.

It was the middle top drawer that was locked.

"I found nothing of interest in the bathroom," Sophie said as she walked into the bedroom and took up a spot behind Kellen. "The usual things were in the medicine cabinet, like antacids and aspirin. There weren't any shaving tools, though. No razor or shaving cream."

"We have a locked drawer," he said as he jiggled it with his right hand. It didn't give.

The sound of keys jingling prompted Kellen to glance over his shoulder. Sophie was checking the doctor's key chain for a small key. "There's no key." She slid the keys back into her jacket pocket. "Hold on, I'll get my lock-picking set."

When he knew she was gone, Kellen grasped the drawer in both hands. He raised it up then tugged hard. The lock broke in seconds.

"I got the kit." Sophie held it up as she moved toward Kellen, but halted a few feet away. He swore he could hear her teeth grinding. "Don't tell me you broke it."

"Okay, I won't."

She moved to his side and glared down at him. "You could get in trouble for that."

"I've never really been one to follow the rules."

"Well then, you're going to get *me* in trouble."

"Nah, you have deniability. You weren't even in the room." He slid the drawer open. It was empty, save for a few utility bills. Kellen picked them up. "Huh. A lock for a few bills? That doesn't make much sense."

"Wait." Sophie snatched the paper from his fingers. "Look at the address. It's not for this place." She folded the paper down to show the name and address on the bill.

"The girlfriend's maybe? If there is one."

She frowned. "If it is, she lives in a really bad part of town. Looks like it's down by the river where there are a bunch of abandoned warehouses. There used to be a big shipping industry in Nouveau Monde, but not anymore. Most of those businesses went bankrupt."

"Let's check it out."

"I'll call Gabe and let him know."

"Okay, but don't let him tell you we can't go." He stood.

She flipped open her cell phone. "If he says we're not going, we're not going."

"Well, maybe *you* can't go, but I'm definitely going. He's not my boss, and even if he was, I'd probably go anyway."

"Are you always this pigheaded?"

He shrugged. "Pretty much. I have to do something, Sophie. Waiting around doing nothing would drive me…well, you know, insane."

She met his gaze and he could tell she was trying to gauge him, trying to figure him out. He could have told her it was pointless. He couldn't even figure himself out. Finally, she nodded and started dialing. "Okay, but

if it comes down to it, I'm saying you kidnapped me
and forced me to take you there."

"Good. That's believable." He grabbed her arm and
pulled her toward the door. "Let's go. You can call him
on the way."

"I don't think this is the girlfriend's place." From the
open front door, Kellen surveyed the apartment. It was
run-down and messy, without the slightest feminine
presence. One bare light bulb hung from the ceiling,
casting a sickly yellow glow over everything. The odor
of mildew and mothballs permeated the air.

On the fourth floor of an abandoned shipping warehouse, the doctor's second home was one large room
separated by those cheaply made, imitation Chinese
room dividers. A torn, putrid green sofa sat in front of
a scarred, oblong wooden table, circa 1970. Piles of
newspapers and magazines were stacked on top of it in
no orderly fashion. Some had slipped off and lay open
on the yellowing tiled floor.

As Kellen moved into the room, he picked up one of
the magazines—*Scientific Journal*. He set it back onto
the table and noticed more of the same. Pawing through
the stack, he saw that they were all scientific magazines,
and the newspapers were from around the world. The
top one was an edition of the *Necropolis Times*, months
old.

A shiver raced down his spine. There was something
ominous about its presence.

"He was definitely living here." Sophie came out of the kitchen area waving a receipt. "It's dated from three days ago. He bought some milk, ketchup, some fruit and vegetables."

Kellen lifted his nose and inhaled. "What's that smell? Chinese food, maybe?"

"There were some take-out containers in the refrigerator. Smells like Chinese."

Frowning, he took another whiff. "Nope, I smell lemon grass, lime maybe. It's Vietnamese. I remember that smell from the war."

"Okay, the doctor likes Vietnamese food. Nothing odd about that."

"No. The odd thing is, why is he living here? Why not at his ridiculously expensive penthouse condo uptown, by his place of work?"

"That is the million-dollar question, Monsieur Falcon."

Kellen smiled at her playful tone and the way she set her hand on her hip. What he wouldn't give to put his hand there—and feel his way around the flare of muscles and over the swell of her rounded rear end. He was losing it again, if he was thinking about touching Sophie instead of concentrating on finding evidence in this case. The case that nearly killed him.

He was definitely walking a fine line between priorities—solving the case or bedding Sophie. Both had equal value right about now, but with his blood starting to race through his veins, bedding Sophie was definitely pulling ahead to the front of the line.

"Hello? Are you still there?" Sophie was standing next to him, waving her hand in front of his face.

"Huh."

"I've been talking to you for the past minute and you were just staring at me without saying anything."

He shook his head, nervous that he'd been able to phase her out with his fantasizing. "Um, sorry. What did you say?"

"You search in here. I'll take the kitchen."

"Okay."

Frowning, she scrutinized his face. "You're sweating again. You're not going to freak out more, are you?"

"Nah. But if I do, you'll be the first to know."

She shook her head. "That's reassuring." But he saw the small smile on her lips before she wandered away to search the kitchen area.

Curious, Kellen moved toward the bookcase along one wall. It was jammed full of books, most of them hardcover scientific texts. As he ran his finger over them, reading the titles, one particular book caught his interest. It was titled *Super Soldiers*. He started to slide it out when something at the edge of his peripheral vision caught his attention.

Turning, he stared at a poster on the wall—*Miss Saigon,* the musical, 1995 Germany tour. The yellow sun was starting to bleed into the red background.

Soon everything around him was bleeding orange.

Shaking his head, he tried to focus on the Vietnamese letter characters on the poster, but it kept shimmering back and forth, as if doing the shimmy to the beat in his head.

The next few moments were a blur to Kellen. He couldn't focus on much, except the thumping in his head. All that was definite to him was that he needed to find Sophie. The urgency stole his breath.

He ran into the kitchen just as she was reaching for a cupboard door. Lightning quick, he snagged her around the waist and half carried, half dragged her toward the big, square windows facing the river. Without a second thought, he pitched them both through the glass.

Right before they hit the roof of the crime scene vehicle that had brought them there, the windows above exploded, raining shards of tempered glass all over them.

Chapter 10

Sophie's wrist throbbed something fierce as she slid the key into the lock on the front door of her house.

The paramedics had announced that she suffered from a few minor bumps and scrapes but nothing hospital-worthy. She was a quick healer, so it didn't surprise her that they didn't press her to go and get X-rays on her wrist. It was just sprained—nothing major. She'd know if she'd broken a bone. She'd broken her leg once when she was a teenager and it had hurt like hellfire. The ache she was experiencing now was nothing in comparison.

Kellen had suffered the worst of the fall. Because of some ingrained sense of chivalry, he had made sure that when they had landed on the car that he buffered her fall with his body.

She glanced over her shoulder and saw how he favored his one leg as he stood waiting for her to open the door. Thankfully, they were under the screened-in porch of her Victorian bungalow. The big elm tree shaded them from the heat of the sun and from prying eyes. Vampires were light-sensitive she knew; some could go hours under the sun's rays without being burned, but Kellen didn't seem to be put out by it. She didn't want to see him in pain, but she hesitated to invite him in. She didn't know why she had suggested bringing him here to begin with.

After the paramedics released them, and Gabriel came by to yell at her for being careless about going to the new address without a police escort so they could clear the building, she should have offered to drive Kellen back to his hotel. Instead, she'd asked if he wanted to come over and have a drink, something she felt they both needed.

"Something wrong with your door?"

She shook her head no, but didn't make a move to open it.

Nodding as if he understood what she was thinking, Kellen wobbled a few steps and sat down on the porch swing with a deep sigh. He reached for her hand, grasped it and pulled her into the swing. She didn't resist when he wrapped his arm around her and cuddled her closely. She liked it that he seemed to know that she needed to be held.

She rested her head against his chest, inhaling his spiced scent. The heat from his body warmed her face.

With every lift of his chest, she heard his heavy intake of air. The hair on her arms and the back of her neck stirred to attention. And her heart picked up speed to match his rising tempo.

Sophie bit back a yawn as she snuggled into Kellen. She felt safe and secure swinging on her porch swing in his arms. Sighing deeply, she took in the smell of the scarlet and dark-purple impatiens planted in several pots around the porch. This spot was one of her favorites, and she came out here to do a lot of her thinking late at night. Not only was it protected from wind, rain and prying eyes by the screens, the ivy that crawled along the mesh made the porch a haven—it was enclosed and safe.

Being next to Kellen, touching him, made her feel invigorated. She'd been seconds away from dying. But he had saved her life by propelling them through a window and down four stories. She'd been in life-threatening situations before, but never anything this close, this out of her control. If Kellen hadn't have been there, she'd be dead. He had sensed the presence of the bomb mere seconds before she triggered it by searching through the cupboards, a task she'd done time and time again as a crime scene investigator.

He'd saved her, but still she was afraid of him. Not afraid of what he could do to her, but how he could make her feel. Being with a vampire was frowned upon by her pack, and she had the one disastrous affair with Jean-Paul; but she couldn't stop the desire thrumming through her body. Nor did she want to.

All she wanted was to revel in her second chance at life.

Kellen stroked her arm with his hand. "Maybe I should go and let you get some sleep. It's been one hell of a day."

"I don't want you to go."

"Sophie, however much I want to be with you, and I really, really do want that, I don't think this is the right time."

"Please don't tell me all the reasons we shouldn't be together. I know them all." Raising her head, she met his gaze. "But I can't stop the feelings inside me. I like being next to you. I like when you touch me. Maybe it's because you snatched me from death that I feel this way. But I don't care, Kellen. I don't care about anything but you and me. Together. Right here, right now."

His eyes widened and his lips parted with a sudden breath. The intensity on his face destroyed any doubt she had about him, any reservation about giving herself to him.

Without waiting for his reply, Sophie pressed her lips to his. Suddenly urgent to taste him, to devour him, she nipped and nibbled on his mouth. He cupped her cheeks and deepened the kiss, parting her lips with a long, thorough sweep of his tongue.

She moaned into him as her tongue matched all his movements, flicking and dipping between his lips. Shivers radiated down her back. Goose bumps rose on her skin. And the tingle between her thighs intensified to a throb that was keeping time to her own heartbeat.

The man could kiss, that was for certain. She'd never felt the zing go from the top of her head to the tips of her toes before. It was forceful and dizzying. Everything around her faded into the background. All she could see, all she could feel, was Kellen.

He made her giddy and frantic. Heat enveloped her like an inferno. Her clothes were too constricting. She needed to shed them immediately or she'd ignite into flames, burning into ashes.

Without breaking contact with his mouth, Sophie tore at her jacket; whimpers of urgency escaped her lips. As if sensing her need or succumbing to his own, Kellen helped her with the rest of her clothing.

He made short work of her shirt by rending it in two with a swift yank of his hands. But she held them still when they attempted to rip off her bra. Deftly, she unclasped the front and tossed it to the side.

"Are you sure about this?" he asked, his eyes glowing a brilliant blue, like a solar eclipse.

"Yes," she panted.

Gripping her around the waist, Kellen lifted her and settled her on his lap with her legs on either side of his thighs. Pressing kisses to her chin, he made his way down her throat, to her collarbone and finally to her breasts. When he sucked one rigid nipple into his wet mouth, her eyes closed in rapture.

His mouth was like heaven on her sweltering skin.

With every draw on her nipple, twin sensations pulled between her thighs. He was pushing her closer and closer to the edge of ecstasy. And she was more than happy to tumble over.

Eager for more, she pushed her breasts into his mouth, urging him on with moans of delight. He suckled at one peak then lavished the same attention on the other, biting down with the edge of his fang. Jolts of pain rushed over her, settling into a smoldering mass of pleasure right at her center. He was driving her mad with the sensual longings he pulled from her body.

Frantic for him, Sophie tore at his T-shirt. Shredded in a matter of seconds, it was little barrier to stop her from stroking her hands over the hard, muscular planes of his chest. She knew he'd be silky smooth under her fingers, and she trailed them over the thick muscles and down the line of his sternum to just below his navel to the waistband of his jeans.

He sucked in a breath as she made short work of the top button on his pants. "Damn, woman, I want you so bad."

"Less talking, more licking," she demanded, as she lifted a breast to his mouth.

With a devilish grin, he obliged her by sucking hard on her pebbled nipple. She wrapped one arm around his neck and let him feast on her flesh. The other hand was busy at the zipper of his jeans. Hungry to feel him in her hand, she slid her fingers through the open gap in his pants and found him, hot and hard.

His moans increased as she, gripping him firmly, stroked his rigid length from base to tip. She rubbed her thumb over his silky smooth head, glorying in the sensations that she felt ripple through him.

Closing his eyes, he bit down on his bottom lip and hissed, "I need to be inside you *now*."

Relinquishing her hold on him, Sophie slid off his lap, then quickly dispatched both her pants and panties. Taking hold of his jeans, she tugged them off with one fast pull and tossed them over her shoulder.

Chuckling, Kellen reached for her, wrapped his hands around her waist and pulled her to him. He pressed an open-mouth kiss to her navel, trailing his tongue over her skin in tiny circles.

"You're incredible," he murmured as he nibbled on her flesh.

Dropping her head back, she reveled in his exploration of her. He kissed and nipped at her hip bones, and dipped his tongue into her belly button. Pleasantly surprised by the way his skin felt under her palms, she rubbed her hands over his head as he discovered her. His velvet-soft hair was an erotic pleasure to experience. And she wondered how it would feel over other parts of her body.

He moved his hands down over her buttocks, feathering his fingertips over the sensitive skin. Circling her inner thighs, he slowly stroked upwards to the heat between them. She sucked in a breath as he slipped his fingers into her, exploring every inch, sliding into every crevice.

Pleasure swirled over her like a tornado. Helpless to

fight it, she let it take her up and spin her around. She clamped onto his head with both hands as he buried two fingers deep inside, filling her, expanding her, preparing her. She was beyond ready. She was already dizzy with the anticipation.

Shuffling forward, Sophie settled one knee onto the swing and beside his leg. Tilting his head back, she looked him in the eyes. "Are you ready for me?"

"From the first second I saw you."

Wrapping one arm around her waist and gripping his cock tight, he guided her onto him. Slowly, torturously, he lowered her. Gritting her teeth against the urge to slam herself down, Sophie dug her fingers into his shoulders and allowed him to lead her, reveling in the delicious torment.

When she was fully seated, he dug his fingers into her hips and found her mouth with his. He kissed her hard, feasting on her lips. Moaning, she returned his fervor and started to grind her pelvis, impatient to find release. An explosive ball of heat throbbed deep inside her. It wouldn't take much for her to go off.

As Sophie glided up and down over him, Kellen thought she was the most enchanting woman he'd ever seen. Like a warrior goddess riding her stallion quick and hard. He had no qualms being the stallion.

Reaching up, he pulled her hair from the elastic tie holding it up, then ran his fingers through the strands as they cascaded down around her shoulders like silken fire. He drank her all in. From the creamy skin of her breasts and her rose-tipped nipples, down her flat belly to the delectable flare of her hips and long muscular legs. She was every inch exquisite and mouthwatering.

And what she was doing to him made him quiver with intense, frantic need. His carnal fantasies paled in comparison to the truth of her, to the reality of the pulse-pounding pleasure surging up and down his body.

Hands pressed over her back, Kellen gathered her close and captured her mouth again to swallow her moans of pleasure. He inhaled them one by one, eager to have more, to push and pound them out of her with every thrust of his cock. He'd bury himself in her completely if he could. Wrap her sweltering form around him and drown in a thousand sultry beads of bliss.

Every time she pushed up with her thighs, Kellen pulled her down, thrusting hard, thrusting deep. He started to feel frenzied, his hunger burning gravely. Blood pounded in his head and he found it difficult to breathe. His climax was close. His thighs were already clenched in anticipation.

Peppering her chin with kisses, he moved down to her throat. Nuzzling at her skin with his nose, he could smell the blood rushing through her veins. He knew she'd taste sweet. He'd only have to pierce the skin with the tip of one fang. Too wrapped up in her own pleasure, she'd never feel it.

Instead, Kellen inhaled Sophie's scent and suckled on her collarbone, reveling in the earthy smell. He'd never break her trust like that. Not for his own selfish need. No—sex with her, feeling every inch of her body, reveling in her heat, was enough to sate him. For once, it would be enough to just have a woman without taking blood.

Sensing her mounting desire, Kellen slid a hand down between them and nestled his knuckles against her most sensitive spot. She ground down on his hand, seeking her release. He wanted more than to give it to her. Hugging her tight with one arm, Kellen drew her up, then slammed her back down as he thrust up to meet her. He kept his hand on her nub, working her with every movement. Pull and push. Up and down. Over and over until sweat poured down and dotted the patterned cushions beneath their writhing bodies. The swing pivoted back and forth, adding to the stimulation.

Unable to hold back any longer, Kellen clamped down on her shoulder, careful of his fangs, and rammed into her, drawing her down to meet him.

"Dieu! Dieu!" Sophie cried, as she fell forward and wrapped one arm around his head and the other over his back, her nails digging into his flesh. She raked them over him as her orgasm plowed into her.

Within his embrace, he could feel her body stiffen and quake, then the glorious rush of liquid heat. Powerless, he clamped his eyes shut and followed her down into orgasmic oblivion.

The intensity overpowered him and he forgot how

to breathe. Sweat dripped into his eyes and he felt like he was drowning. Everything went black, then white, then black again. The force of his orgasm scared him, and he lifted his head to find air and steady himself.

The porch was reeling. He felt light-headed, intoxicated. He usually loved the euphoric sensation, but fear—fear of letting Sophie get too close—needled its way in and made him dizzy instead.

Gripping her waist, he lifted her off of him and set her down on the swing. He stood, but his legs were unsteady and he fell back again, sending the swing into motion.

"What's wrong?" she asked, and he could hear the hurt in her voice.

He didn't want to see it in her face.

He stood again and reached for his jeans. He put them on without looking at her. He felt like a jerk for acting this way, but he couldn't calm the panic inside him. Was it the disease acting up again? Or was he just such a coward he couldn't deal with the overwhelming emotions he was feeling right now?

"Look at me."

He stopped trying to piece his shirt together and looked at her. Her skin was flushed and sweaty. Her hair was like a fiery curtain framing an amazing face. God, she was breathtaking. It staggered him completely. And that was why he was panicking. She was doing to him what no woman had ever come close to achieving. His armor was down and he was falling headfirst into an emotional world he knew nothing about.

"Don't make me regret this, Kellen Falcon. Don't you dare."

"I'm sorry." He lifted a shaky hand, surprised at the fine tremble he felt, to try to touch her—then lowered it, unsure of himself. "It was great. You're great."

She stood and he could see the beginning spark of fury in her eyes. But it was the tears welling in the corners that had his knees wobbling. He'd be okay if she just didn't cry.

"I'm great? Well, that's just lovely. Thank you so very much."

Bunching her hands into fists, she pushed past him, and forgetting her clothes, she opened her front door, went in and slammed it shut.

He didn't know how long he stood on her porch and stared at the closed door. He knew he should go to her, reassure her. He took a step forward, but stopped, one hand on the knob. Slowly turning around, his shoulders hunched down, uncertain, he walked away instead, feeling as though his feet were made of lead.

By the time he flagged down a taxi and made it back to his hotel room he was cold and numb. But he didn't think it had anything to do with the refreshing night air.

Chapter 11

Insomnia forced Kellen from his hotel room. He'd been doing nothing but pacing the room, with the television, its sound off, flickering in the background. He had too much on his mind, with no avenue to express it.

Walking the streets didn't help, either. It proved to be more detrimental than helpful, especially in his state of mind. The clubs and bars near the hotel were hopping, crowds of people swarming on the sidewalks to get in. The last thing he needed was a few drinks and too many enticements.

He'd been propositioned three times in a span of two blocks, and it was getting harder to resist. Maybe if he gave in, he'd forget the feel of Sophie wrapped around his body. Sure, and maybe the virus running through his veins would just disappear.

A dark-haired beauty strolled down the sidewalk toward him, her gaze and smile sending an invitation that was impossible to miss. The old Kellen would have accepted without a second thought.

Instead, he had whistled for a taxi and had taken it down to the wharf, to the last bomb site. Maybe picking through burnt debris and rubble would ease his mind, by focusing it on something other than Sophie. The crime scene team had most likely collected what seemed important and taken it to the lab to be analyzed, but he had to do something. He'd go mad otherwise.

Yellow police tape still roping off the area fluttered in the breeze. The wharf seemed deserted except for the rats and other scavengers, which is what Kellen sort of felt like. Ducking under the tape, he walked around the warehouse, glancing up at the shattered fourth-story windows that he and Sophie jumped out of.

They'd been lucky that he could sense the bomb before it went off. Sophie would have definitely been killed, and he would have suffered some injuries, but probably not enough to kill him. Vampires were a lot harder to kill than lycans. Either their hearts or their heads had to be severed.

If Sophie had died, it would have seemed like that had happened anyway.

Stopping under the windows, he searched the ground

for debris from the doctor's apartment. Because of his superior night vision, he didn't need a flashlight. He toed over pieces of blackened wood and metal, looking for anything that looked interesting or deserved a second inspection. Nothing jumped out at him.

He moved toward the main entrance, hoping the stairs were still intact and stable. He started up, eyeing each step as he went—not only for evidence but to make sure they were solid and able to support his weight. The last thing he needed right about now was to fall through the stairs and break something.

After reaching the fourth floor, Kellen cautiously moved toward the doctor's ruined apartment. The one wall with the door was intact and Kellen slowly pushed it open. The bare living room he'd stood in earlier that day was now littered with burnt wood chunks, plastic pieces and other debris. The sofa was still recognizable, as was the table; but the bookcase had been blasted apart into several chunks, the books upon it shredded into kitty litter.

A lot of the debris, he imagined, had already been picked up and carted over to the lab. But Gabriel and Olena hadn't been there to see what had piqued Kellen's interest to begin with. The book on super soldiers. That was his main objective. To find it, or at least pieces of it that he could put together later at the lab.

As he moved through the room he scanned the floor

searching for something, anything resembling that book or anything possibly related to it. The floor creaked as he walked. He imagined some of the boards had been weakened by the explosion. Cautious, he set his foot down, listening for any sign that it would give under his weight. When it didn't groan, he took another step and then another, until he was standing where the bookcase would have been. A long board, partially intact, lay along the damaged wall, separating the living room from the kitchen, where the explosion had originated.

Crouching, Kellen lifted up the board. Underneath, he found a piece of what he was looking for. The thick book had been bound in black leather. What he found was half of the cover and about fifty pages, cut in half, still clinging to the spine.

After picking it up, he stood and flipped through the remaining pages. Some were charred, the text illegible, but others he could decipher with no problem.

He wasn't a scientist, but from what he could discern just from the cursory examination, the content of the book revolved around genetics and blood disorders. Some of the ripped pages had handwritten notes penciled in the margins—the doctor's thoughts and questions about the information in the text. Some of the notes made Kellen's skin crawl.

"Test subjects for immunity."

"Superior strength? Blood-related?"

"Find right kind of chemical to mix with vampire blood."

It appeared the good doctor was doing more than his civic duty during the war.

Angry, Kellen turned the book over, intent on taking it with him, to go through it back at his hotel room, when the last notation caused his blood to run cold.

"Administer with the hep A vaccine."

Squeezing his eyes tight against the onslaught of thoughts raging through his mind, Kellen remembered a time in Vietnam when he had fallen ill…the one and only time he'd ever been sick in his life.

He was back in the Da Nang army base for the weekend. After two weeks of humping it through thick jungle along the Ho Chi Minh trail, their captain insisted that the company needed some R & R. Kellen was looking forward to a long nap, a few bottles of cold beer and a chance to win back some of the money he'd lost playing poker the last time he was there. But first he had to report to the medic, to have his routine physical.

He could have told them to stop wasting their time with their lame tests. They would never find anything wrong with him. Being a vampire meant he'd never suffer illness, at least not the human kind. But to confess that would be to "out" himself, and he didn't think the world was quite ready to hear that the creatures of myths, nightmares and B horror movies actually lived among the rest of civilization. And quite comfortably at that.

There were a few other soldiers milling about when he entered the medical building. He nodded to a couple, saluted a sergeant and then wandered into the room where he was supposed to meet the doctor. A pretty nurse he'd never seen before waited for him instead.

She turned when he entered, and smiled. "Good morning, Private Falcon."

"Morning. Where's the doc?" He jumped up onto the examining table.

"I'll be doing your exam. You don't mind, do you?" She smiled at him again, pulling the cloth curtain closed.

"Don't mind at all." Sliding off the table, Kellen shed his clothes.

After the examination—Kellen had thoroughly enjoyed the nurse's warm, petite hands on his body, instead of the cool, hairy hands of the regular doctor— while he was getting dressed, the nurse came back with a needle. She tapped the end to rid it of air bubbles, then proceeded to rub alcohol on Kellen's arm with a cotton swab.

"Whoa! What's that?"

"Vaccination."

"I don't need it." He tried to move his arm, but she held it tight. Tighter than he would have expected from a woman so small and compact.

"Everyone needs it."

There was something in her eyes that gave Kellen pause. Staring at her, he released some of his power, getting a sense of her. Maybe she was an Otherworlder and he had just missed it the first time because he was so used to being the only one out there in the war.

After a sweep of her form, he confirmed that she was indeed human. But still, something lingered on her that gave him pause. Something different.

"What type of vaccination?"

"Hepatitis A and B. It runs rampant out here, especially with all the gallivanting you boys seem to be doing in and out of the field."

Not wanting to alert her to his Otherness, he nodded and let her give him the shot. It wouldn't do any harm anyway. To his system, it would be as if she injected him with water.

"There. That wasn't so bad, was it?" She slid the needle out and stroked his arm. "Now you can play all you want." After another wide smile, she slipped past the curtain. He watched her shadow walk away, then finished getting dressed.

That night in his bunk, after losing a bunch of money in poker again, Kellen got sick. Really sick. Something that had never happened to him before.

Pain ripped through his body. It was like being whipped by a rope of fire over and over again. A great burning started at his feet and made its way up his body to his head, searing every nerve ending along the way.

Twisting and writhing in his bunk, his clothes and blankets soaked with his sweat, Kellen thought he was going to die. He begged whatever benevolent god that would listen to let him. White spots blinded his vision and he threw up until his stomach was empty. Still he retched, until his throat tore open and he was spitting up blood.

A few of his bunk mates gathered around him, eyes glassed over, unsure of what to do. Until finally, after one long shudder of his body and a final stab of pain in his gut, Kellen's body gave out and he fell unconscious.

The next morning he woke in the infirmary, feeling rested and invigorated. The nurse looking after him had told him that he had been running a one-hundred-and-eight temperature for most of the night, but now he was back to normal. She'd never seen anything like it.

After checking his vitals again, she pronounced him healthy, then handed him a box wrapped in brown crepe paper. "This was left for you."

He ripped off the wrapping to reveal a beautiful wood box, covered with red silk, with black grasshoppers embroidered on the cloth. He opened it. It was empty inside but it had been inlaid with bone. It was a gift of exquisite workmanship. There was no note with it to say who it was from. But he thought he knew.

Feeling strangely elated, Kellen remembered searching the medical facility for the young nurse that had given him the shot. He wanted to know what she really had given him. But he couldn't find her, and never saw her again after that day.

A low groaning noise shot Kellen back to reality. Reacting much too slowly, he tried to move off the area he'd been standing on. But it proved to be too late.

The floor beneath him caved in.

Tucking the book beneath his armpit, Kellen leaped to the side, managing to one-hand-grasp the floorboards to keep from dropping four stories into a pit of broken wood. Although the fall wouldn't injure him, impaling himself on something sharp wouldn't be a good thing. Negligence and stupidity were two ways he really didn't want to depart from his mortal coil.

He pulled himself up, and rolled onto his back to a safe part of the floor. At least, he hoped it was safe. For now, it wasn't breaking apart. Getting to his feet, he realized that a gaping, jagged hole prevented him from reaching the door.

He moved toward the blasted-out windows and looked down at the ground, searching for anything that could injure him if he landed on it. Nothing seemed to be sticking out. Taking a deep breath, he jumped and landed safely on the ground.

Brushing at the soot and dirt on his jeans, Kellen glanced around at the area. Everything was dark and deserted. He was going to have to walk for a while before finding a taxi. He didn't mind. He got what he came for. Evidence that Dr. Bueller was not who he seemed—and that there was a connection between him and the doctor.

Chapter 12

As Sophie shuffled through the photos from the medical center surveillance, another wave of anger surged over her. She slammed the pictures down on the table and rubbed at her stinging eyes.

Her eyes hurt from crying. Like an idiot, she had sobbed after Kellen had left. Both angry and hurt, she hadn't been able to stem the flow of tears. If she could have she would have taken out her frustration on a punching bag. Preferably one that looked exactly like Kellen Falcon.

She felt more embarrassed than anything that she had succumbed to her desire and had sex with another vampire—something she swore she would never do again, even if the vampire in question was the most alluring man she'd ever laid eyes on. And here came a cocky, smooth-talking, borderline insane one, and she submitted after only two days of knowing him. She felt like a fool. She hoped Gabriel never found out. He'd be extremely disappointed by her behavior.

And if her father ever found out, he'd certainly disown her, maybe even shame her out of the pack.

Gabriel took that very moment to stalk into the room with his arms full of evidence from the second bombing. He set down the heavy canister, filled with what she knew to be debris from Dr. Bueller's second residence, onto the far table. "Any matches to our briefcase?"

She gestured to a small stack of photos on the table. "About twenty matches so far."

"With our patient photo list we're compiling, it should be easy going after that."

She nodded, but refused to meet his gaze.

He leaned on the table next to her and frowned. "Is there something you need to tell me?"

"No."

"Where's Kellen? He should be here to go through this stuff."

"How the hell should I know?" she growled.

"Didn't you take him home last night?"

Her head came up at that, and she could feel her face redden. "What is that supposed to mean?"

Straightening, he stared at her, his brow furrowed. "Sophie?"

It was just one word, but she knew what he was asking her. He knew. It was probably written all over her face and body language. The inspector was a trained investigator and a lycan to boot. There was no hiding something like this from him. But still she refused to say anything.

She lowered her gaze and put her attention back onto the photos. "I'll be done with these soon."

Sighing, he rubbed a hand over his face, but didn't press her any further. "Okay, I'm going to track down Kellen and get him to work on this second bomb." Then he sighed again. "Do I need to take him off his case? I'll do it if you're having…issues."

She shook her head while thumbing through the pictures absently. Anything to keep her hands busy and stop them from shaking with anger. "I'm fine."

"All right." He headed for the door then stopped. "Well, speak of the devil."

Sophie tensed. She knew the second Kellen stepped into the room. Something shifted over her skin, something alien but not unpleasant. She shivered and had to dig her nails into the palm of her hand to stop from swinging around in her chair to greet him.

"You look like hell, boy," Gabriel muttered. "Didn't sleep well?"

"Something like that."

Sophie could hear the weariness in his voice, but she stifled the urge to turn.

"What's with all the vultures out front? It was hard to even get into the building."

"Yeah, the media are camped out looking for anything to feed to the masses. The terrorist story is starting to cause a mass panic in the city."

She didn't look up, but she knew he moved into the room and was standing by Gabriel. Her nostrils flared in response to his scent floating in the air.

Damn it! Why hadn't she been more careful? Now that they had slept together, she'd always respond to him, to his smell, to his voice. There were consequences to taking that step. She was suffering through them right now. The big difference was, she'd never experienced them this strongly with anyone before. She'd expect it with another lycan, but not ever with a vampire.

"I retrieved what I could from the doctor's second residence. Can you go through it and see if you can piece together the bomb and anything else you might find?"

"I'm on it."

"Good," Gabriel said, then left the room.

Sophie busied herself with the pictures as Kellen walked over to the far table. She forced her head down, but it didn't last. She looked at him as he put on gloves and lifted the top off the heavy plastic tub the inspector had brought in.

He did look awful. Even from where she sat, she could see the dark circles under his eyes and the sallow pallor of his skin. When he glanced up and met her gaze, she could also clearly see red lines in the whites of his eyes.

He half smiled at her, his cockiness stripped, leaving only a vulnerable man behind. He appeared confused and uncertain as he looked at her.

She didn't want to feel any sympathy, but it seeped into her heart regardless of her efforts to trample it down.

"Gabe's right, you look terrible." She set the photos on the table.

"Must be jet lag." He started picking out fragments of different materials from the bucket and placing them on the work area in front of him.

Despite her anger, she stood and walked over to him. When she neared, she could see the sheen on his forehead. Sweat was beading over his skin. She didn't find it hot in the room at all. In fact, she had been tempted to retrieve a sweater from her locker in the staff quarters.

She put her hand on his arm and was nearly seared. His skin was blistering. "You're feverish." She set her palm on his forehead and on the back of his neck. "Have you taken blood lately?"

Leaning into her touch, he shook his head. "I haven't had a chance."

"Idiot têtu."

"Would you quit calling me names? Especially in French. It reminds me too much of my mother."

"Well, you deserve it." She guided him to a chair in the corner. "Sit. I'll get you something to drink."

She rushed out of the room, down the hall and into the staff room. A vending machine stood along one wall. Digging out change from her jean pockets, she fed some coins into the machine and pushed the button. A plastic bottle of blood fell into the tray. She took it out and rushed back into the work room.

Twisting off the cap, she handed it to Kellen. "It's O negative. I hope that's okay. I didn't know what you preferred."

He took the offered drink and downed it in two big gulps. When he was done, he shut his eyes and let his head fall back with a sigh of satisfaction. "Thank you." He opened his eyes and looked at her. Despite the redness, his eyes sparkled like blue diamonds.

"Is it the disease?"

"I don't know."

She chewed her bottom lip. "Is that why you freaked out on me?"

Lifting his head, he reached for her hand. "I don't know. Possibly."

"You don't know much, do you?"

Touching him again sent shivers racing over her body. She wanted to crawl into his lap and wrap her arms around him. Licking her lips, she thought of the way he had kissed her, the way he had touched her. Her thighs tingled with the memory of it.

She hated that her attraction to him hadn't dulled. Their lovemaking had only increased her desire for him. Even if he hurt her afterward, her body responded to him. It was her heart that held back. Her heart *and* her mind. Her body had always been the treacherous one.

"Sophie, I—"

Olena burst into the room. "We have a few possible suspects. Gabriel wants to see everyone in the conference room right away."

Kellen dropped Sophie's hand and stood. Sophie turned her attention to Olena. The vampiress was eyeing them with one elegant eyebrow raised.

"Oh, did I interrupt something scandalous?"

Sophie shook her head, her throat tight and unable to form words, then she walked out of the room without looking back.

Chapter 13

Kellen slid into one of the chairs at the conference table, trying hard not to stare at Sophie. Already seated at the end, she hadn't glanced in his direction when he had walked into the room. Her regret was palpable, like a curtain of electricity, and he desperately wanted to soothe it away but wasn't sure if she'd let him.

He had so many things he wanted to say to her. First off was an apology for acting the fool after they had sex. It had been an explosive event for him and he still wasn't comfortable with the emotions swirling in him, but he knew he had hurt her, and for that he was sorry. She didn't deserve his erratic and distant behavior.

But he had no idea what to say to make up for that. Was it even possible to make up for acting so callously?

He also wanted to tell her about the book he found last night. And about the memory that nearly drowned him, about Vietnam. Crazy as it might sound, he strongly suspected that there was a connection between him, his experience in the war and Dr. Bueller.

Gabriel stood at the front of the room, a stack of files sitting in front of him on the table. "Here's our update so far: the investigation into NORM is slow-going. The human authorities are binding us with a bunch of ridiculous red tape. The receptionist has been thoroughly questioned, and it looks like she is in the clear. All of the deceased were investigated, and they are all in the clear, too. So that still leaves us with no viable suspects." He patted the stack of folders. "After some digging, we found out that Dr. Bueller had quite a few malpractice suits against him." He flipped open the first file folder. "Some of these cases are ten years old, but a few are more recent."

"Maybe one of them got impatient and decided to take matters into his own hands," Sophie added.

"Exactly what I was thinking." Gabriel tapped his pen on the table. "And after Sophie and Kellen discovered that the doctor may be living a dual life, I'd say we've got a very interesting case on our hands."

"What do you want us to do?" Olena asked.

"I want you and Sophie to cross-reference these files with the current patient records, and the surveillance photos François printed out for us. Maybe we'll get lucky and find a match." He looked at Kellen. "I want you to keep putting the second bomb together. If they are the same type, maybe we can track this guy from the components."

"I'd also like to look deep into the doctor's background," Kellen said.

Gabriel raised a brow. "You know something I don't?"

"No," he lied. "Just a feeling."

After a thorough look over, the inspector finally nodded. "Okay, I'll go with that because your last 'feeling' saved Sophie, which I appreciate."

Sophie glanced at him then, and the floor nearly fell out from beneath him again. He wanted to reach across the table and grasp her hand, touch her face, anything to make a connection again. For as much as they had been linked earlier, he could feel her slipping away from him. Although he wasn't sure if he wanted her for keeps, he certainly needed her for now.

Gabriel slid the folders down the table toward Sophie and Olena. "That's it for now. Let's hope we have something by the end of the day. A suspect to question would be nice."

Kellen watched as Sophie gathered the files, then stood and exited the room. Reluctantly, he stood and followed. Olena walked beside him, wrapping her hands around his arm.

"You look like someone ripped your heart out," she said, her eyes twinkling with her secret knowledge.

"Haven't you heard? I don't have a heart."

She chuckled. "Hmm, I think you like to pretend you don't. But it's there. Pumping hard. Yearning for what it may not have."

They stood in front of the workroom. Sophie was already inside, busy going through files. Kellen's gaze automatically tracked her from across the room. She was like a flame that lit up his darkness and made life easier.

"It will take a lot to tame the wild beast," Olena said, breaking him out of his reverie. Kellen looked at the vampiress. "If you really want her, it will take more than just your sexual prowess. That girl needs patience, trust and love. If you're willing to put that out, you might just have a chance." Smiling, she patted his arm and then went into the room to help Sophie with the files.

Love? What the hell did Kellen know about love? Nothing. He wasn't even sure he loved his mother. She hadn't been an easy person to love, always full of unkind words and a cruel disciplinary hand.

He could definitely offer Sophie trust, possibly patience, even if he did have images of her naked body constantly in his mind. But love? He hadn't been planning on anything that problematic. Not with the way he was. Not with the disease inside his bloodstream slowly destroying his mind. What kind of relationship could he honestly give her, knowing his days were numbered?

Rubbing his head, he thought maybe it was best that they had ended before they ever truly began. He couldn't offer her any more than he'd already given. A few nights of good sex was about all he could muster. He had problems, and the last thing he wanted was to hurt anyone. Especially someone like Sophie—someone he was really starting to care for. Despite his aversion to emotion, he possessed a wide range of them for her. It was strange and frightening for him because he didn't really know if it was solely because of her effect on him, or if the *Sangcerritus* was in overdrive, upping the pace to devour his mind.

Either way, the best thing for them both was for Kellen to keep his thoughts and his hands to himself.

He walked into the room, his head forward, resisting the urge to look at Sophie, and went to work on reconstructing the second bomb. The sooner he could help solve this case, the sooner he could move on and do what he had come to Nouveau Monde to do—find a cure to his affliction or die trying.

After a couple of hours, Kellen had put together the second bomb. It had been an easier task than the first one, because he suspected the bomb would be the same. And it had been, except for the outer casing, because it had been stashed in a cupboard. The timer, a gold watch this time, had started the moment they had entered the doctor's residence. But the construction of the IED had been exactly the same.

He'd been able to work in relative peace and quiet, as Olena and Sophie had taken their tasks to another room. However much he liked watching Sophie move, he'd been thankful for the reprieve.

Now that the bomb had been reconstructed, Kellen was intent on digging into Dr. Bueller's background. The bombs, the doctor's secret hideaway and the books on his shelves were connected. The *Miss Saigon* poster also rubbed him raw. He didn't really peg the doctor for a big musical fan. He could be wrong, but something about it gave him pause. Had the doctor been in Vietnam?

After a thorough search through city documents, Kellen found files like banking information, phone records and background checks on Dr. Jonathon Bueller. But nothing alerted him to anything out of the ordinary. According to the records they had access to, the doctor never served in the army of any country.

Using the World Wide Web, Kellen searched for any other information he could uncover. What he discovered was a number of articles about research on his blood disease, the same ones Kellen had found with his search on *Sangcerritus* before coming to France, and a website about his medical practice. He'd need to dig into genealogy to find what he was hoping to unearth.

He'd have to ask Gabriel if they had access to a genealogy department in the city. He wanted a lineage search, since the doctor didn't have a wife, kids, or any next of kin listed. For a vampire, it wasn't abnormal, as he'd outlive everyone—except if he had married and procreated with another vampire, which in itself was extremely rare. Or if he had been successful in turning someone. But so far, all the evidence pointed to nothing of the sort. As far as Kellen could tell, no one knew the doctor all that well.

Standing and twisting out the kinks from sitting so long, Kellen left the workroom to go locate Gabriel. He'd try the inspector's office, the lab, and then the other workrooms. He'd avoid the one in which he knew Sophie and Olena were likely still to be working. He wasn't quite ready to see Sophie again. Diving into work had exorcised her from his mind, at least for a while; but now that he was roaming around the offices, hands and mind free, his thoughts had strayed to her again.

He was definitely in a bad way.

Striding down the hall, he poked his head into Gabriel's office but didn't find the inspector. He was walking toward the lab when he heard Gabriel's voice from around the corner.

With the question already on his lips, he turned the corner but pulled up sharp when he saw who the inspector was talking to—the lycan cop who had been around Sophie earlier.

"Kellen." Gabriel almost looked nervous, as his gaze flitted from the lycan back to Kellen.

"I was wondering if you had access to genealogy," Kellen asked, trying hard to avoid the way the other lycan was glaring at him, nostrils flaring.

"Yes, we do."

"I was just looking for you, vampire."

Kellen glanced at the bigger lycan and pointed to himself. "You're looking for me?"

Gabriel cleared his throat. "Kellen, this is Constable Duncan Quinn."

Ignoring the inspector's introduction, Duncan moved toward Kellen, his meaty hands fisted at his sides. "I have a few words to say to you."

"Yes?"

"Stay away from Sophie."

He supposed he should have sensed the lycan's jealousy the moment he came upon him. He decided to play the fool. "I'm sorry?"

"The word around is that you're flirting with her."

Kellen smiled. It never failed to amaze him how fast gossip could travel. "Ah, well, you see, I think that's up to Sophie, don't you think?"

Duncan stepped into Kellen's space, puffing his chest out like a gorilla. "No, that's where you're wrong, vampire. It's up to members of her pack like me to ask you, nice and polite, to stay away from her."

Kellen shook his head when what he really wanted to do was send this guy sailing across the hall. "It amazes me how you ever managed to evolve."

"What did you say?" Duncan stared down Kellen.

"You're acting like a Neanderthal."

"Are you calling me names, bloodsucker?"

Gabriel took that moment, finally, to step in. "Look, Duncan, this isn't the time or place to solve this. Cool down and go for a walk."

"Stay out of this, Gabriel. This is between me and the freak here."

"Freak, huh?" Kellen gave him a sardonic half smile. "So says the man that turns all hairy and barks like a dog at the sight of a full moon."

Duncan obviously didn't enjoy Kellen's sense of humor as much as Kellen did.

The lycan poked Kellen in the chest with one meaty finger. "Don't mouth off to me, little man."

As quick as lightning, Kellen had Duncan by the throat and was backing him up down the hall. Surprised, the lycan tore at Kellen's hand with distended claws. It didn't faze Kellen. He couldn't even feel it as his flesh was ripped open and blood rushed down his forearm. He had only one thought: to hurt Duncan Quinn.

The big man kicked at Kellen's legs with punishing blows and swung at his head with beefy fists made for bruising. Every solid connection just amped up Kellen's anger until he could see nothing but red. Literally. It was if the world had been bathed in blood. He could even smell it all around him. Hunger twisted his stomach.

Glaring into the lycan's face, Kellen felt like breaking the man's neck. Duncan's face was starting to turn purple, his eyes bugging out. Swiveling, Kellen tossed Duncan up against a wall. The impact cracked the wallboard.

Leaning into Duncan's face, Kellen hissed, "Who's the little man now?"

He didn't hear Sophie approach, but he felt her hand on his arm. The warmth from her palm penetrated the crimson fog in his mind. Slowly, he could feel his fury seeping away, like a small leak in a balloon.

"Kellen, let him go," she ordered.

Puffing through his nostrils, Kellen tried to slow the adrenaline rushing through his system. He unhooked his fingers from Duncan's neck and moved away.

The lycan slumped down the wall to the floor, rubbing at his bruised throat. He coughed and sucked in air, coughing even more.

Kellen didn't look at Duncan but at Sophie, who stood next to him. She was examining his shredded hand. "Are you okay?"

"Is *he* okay?" Duncan barked. "What about me? That psychopath nearly killed me."

Gabriel was there, holding his hand out to Duncan to help him to his feet. "He didn't kill you, Duncan."

"I want to press charges. You saw him attack me."

"I saw you provoke him, big guy. So let's just call it an even split. If he had killed you, I would've definitely arrested him."

Duncan pushed Gabriel's helping hand away and glared at Sophie. "I can't believe you care about this guy. He's a freaking nut job. Look at his eyes! They're as red as blood."

Kellen watched Sophie's face as her gaze fell from his. Was there a blush on her cheeks from embarrassment?

More anger was starting to flare inside him. He needed to get away before he did something unforgivable.

Turning on his heel, he strode down the hall. Sophie called after him, but he didn't stop. His strides turned quicker and soon he was running.

Chapter 14

It didn't take Sophie long to track Kellen down. His cinnamon scent was distinctive and strong, especially in his emotional state.

She had followed it through the lab, out the front doors, down the street and to the tree-lined park adjacent to the main building. She'd spent many evenings in the park, running through the thick woods in her wolf form. This was where she came to think and cool off.

Except, Kellen wasn't running off his fury. Instead, he stood *in* the big stone fountain, jets of water streaming over his head.

As she neared, she could almost see steam rising from his body as the cool liquid hit him. It must have been a trick of the light, or the heat of the sun, because that couldn't be possible. A man, vampire or not, couldn't run that hot—could he? Maybe the disease had increased his body temperature.

He didn't turn to face her, but she sensed he knew she had approached. It was in the way his shoulders bunched and his breathing increased.

She sat on the edge of the fountain, the fine mist of the water hitting her face. "That's an interesting way to cool off." She glanced around and noticed that no one else seemed to be in the park. At least, not where they were situated.

He shrugged but still hadn't turned to look at her. "Since I can't shift and run it off…I thought, what the hell?"

She laughed despite herself. Kellen looked way too good soaking wet. His T-shirt clung sinuously to his muscular build. She had to divert her attention somehow. Laughter seemed like a good option.

Until he turned and looked at her.

The laughter died on her lips and she had an urge to retreat. He looked feral, completely on the edge of himself. His eyes were on fire and they burned a path right through to her soul.

Nervous, she fidgeted with one of the buttons on her blouse. "I'm sorry about Duncan. He had no right to talk to you about me."

"Don't apologize for him."

"Okay, I won't." She risked a glance at him. He still

stood in the rush of water, gazing down at her. His teeth weren't even chattering. The man must have been impervious to the cold. She wished she was just as impervious to the way he was looking at her, as if he really wanted to eat her whole. Shivers raced up and down her arms and legs at the thought of that. Would he start at her toes, lavishing attention on every inch of her flesh?

"What are you doing here?" he asked, his voice rough, husky.

"I was…concerned about you."

"Well, maybe it would be best for everyone if you weren't."

She stood, the sting of his words digging into her heart. To think she'd come out here worried about him, hoping that he would somehow allow her to comfort him. She'd been a fool to think he'd permit her that much. It would mean that he'd have to admit a weakness, and Kellen would sooner shift into a wolf than allow that he was vulnerable.

"Yes, I can see that now. I was an idiot to think otherwise."

He clenched a fist, then relaxed. "Look, Sophie, I'm sorry. I can't be whatever it is you want me to be. Maybe Duncan's right and we have no business being together."

Those words, more than any others, slashed her to the bone. She shouldn't have been surprised, though. Didn't she just say the same thing to him earlier? That they couldn't be together because he was a vampire and she was a lycan? She wished she could tell him that she had slept with him because of who he was, not what he was. But she wasn't sure he'd believe her.

"That's it, then? That's all you have to say to me?"

"No, that's not it." He stepped toward her, his expression unreadable. He grabbed her arm and pulled her up into the fountain. The movement was so quick, his grasp so powerful, that she nearly slipped when her feet finally touched the stone. She reached for him and he wrapped his arms around her, bringing his mouth down to hers. He kissed her hard, with hot, wet lips.

She was helpless to do anything but hold onto him as he feasted on her mouth. The jet of water gushed over them, but she didn't care. She was oblivious to it. She was oblivious to everything but Kellen.

Digging her fingers into his chest, tempted to tear at the wet shirt clinging to him, she kissed him back just as hard, just as fierce. She wanted him more than any man before. The intensity of it punched her in the stomach and she lost her breath.

She came up for air as Kellen pressed kisses to her chin and down over her throat, nibbling and licking her wet skin. She was shaking, but it was more than just the coolness of the water sluicing over her that caused her quivers. Desire, hot and hearty, surged through her like molten silver and pained her just as much. It made her feel both exhilarated and terrified. To feel so much about one person unnerved her. Especially a man like Kellen—someone she knew had no intention of sticking around for long, whether of his own accord or by the life-threatening disease racing through his system.

He had hurt her once. Could she stand another piece of her heart being chipped away? Because it was inevitable that he would in the end. He made it obvious that he was here for only a short while. That this was a detour.

Her hands pressed against his chest, Sophie pulled her mouth from his. There were things she wanted to say, but she didn't have the right words. She wasn't sure if there *were* right words.

Sighing, he rested his forehead against hers, but didn't make a move to let her go.

"You'll hurt me again."

"I don't want to, Sophie." His voice was just a whisper.

"I know, but you will. You won't be able to help it."

He moved his hands up her back, then around to cup her face with his palms. Dipping his head, he looked her deep in the eyes. She felt like drowning in the illuminated blue depths.

With eyes open, he touched her lips with his and murmured against them. "You destroy me, Sophie St. Clair." After another brushing of his lips, he let her go and took a step back.

Finding it difficult to breathe, Sophie turned away from him and stepped out of the fountain. Water sloshed in her shoes as she trudged back across the park toward the lab. She wrapped her arms around her body to stem the shivers that erupted over her.

Luckily, she had another change of clothing in her

locker, but she wasn't sure what she could do to stop the cold rushing over her. It had nothing to do with the wind against her wet skin, and everything to do with Kellen's parting words.

Kellen didn't want to watch Sophie walk away, but he couldn't tear his gaze from her as she moved across the grass toward the lab, arms wrapped around her torso. He was an idiot for pulling her into the fountain. What was he thinking? Or maybe the problem was that he wasn't thinking. His only thoughts had been about kissing and touching her. Selfish, arrogant thoughts, with no mind to what was best for her or what she needed.

How he ended up in the fountain in the first place boggled him. The last thing he could truly remember was walking down the hall, searching for Gabriel. Then everything blurred after that. He knew he had run into Duncan, and the lycan cop had words with him. Harsh words, if Kellen could recall, warning him away from Sophie. Then the lycan had touched him. Something had snapped inside Kellen's mind.

All he could think about was how hot he had been. Burning from the inside out, it had seemed. His vision had been red and hazy, and Kellen thought he desperately needed something to cool him down. The breeze outside had done nothing to help. But when he had spotted the water jetting from the large stone fountain, he knew that was where he should go. Jumping into it had not been a conscious thought.

Then he sensed Sophie approaching him, and he had heard her voice, and everything came crashing down around him. He became hyperaware of what he had done.

He had looked at her, staring up at him, her eyes flaring angrily, and his one thought had been to touch her, to taste her sensuous mouth. After that, his mind had blacked out and emotion took over. Wild, feral emotions that were starting to overcome him. Anger, hunger, lust. They were his constant companions. It was as if he was going through his initial vampire transition again; lost, confused and unpredictable.

He was a danger to Sophie. Beyond the fact that they were from different species, and her pack had certain rules, he was no good for her. He didn't want to hurt her, not emotionally, and definitely not physically. If something happened to her he'd never forgive himself. For once in his life, he actually considered the consequences of his actions.

And it didn't feel particularly welcome in his body. To make room for a conscience, he had to part with other things, like recklessness and carelessness. What if he missed them? Could he get them back?

Kellen jumped out of the fountain. A few people were milling about the park, watching him from a wary distance. He didn't blame them. He was becoming wary of himself. His episodes were becoming more frequent. And he was finding it more difficult to control the results. He knew a time would come when he'd be completely unaware of his actions. Only the disease pumping through his veins would be in charge.

Wringing out the water from his shirt, Kellen trudged across the grass and toward the main building. He hoped they had dryers in the men's washroom that he could use. He could just imagine what Gabriel was going to say. He'd be surprised if the inspector didn't kick him off the case and send him packing back to America.

Maybe that was what he should do. It wasn't really his case. He didn't work for the Nouveau Monde crime unit. He was visiting as a civilian and just happened to be in an explosion that killed the doctor he had been hoping to see. It's not like he knew the man.

Kellen stopped walking. Something didn't add up. There was something peculiar about the doctor's secret apartment. Closing his eyes, he tried to picture the guy's place before it blew. Images of the living room skipped by. The stacks of magazines and newspapers came to his mind. It was strange and obsessive in itself. But there had been something, hadn't there? Something that pricked Kellen's mind as odd, even eerie.

The newspapers.

The top one was a *Necropolis Times*. Why would the doctor have a paper from Necropolis?

He squeezed his eyes tighter, trying to recall the paper's headline. There had been a picture. In the photo there had been a group of people. The caption read: *Necropolis's Finest Save the City from Ruin.*

It was a story about the crime scene unit, and Kellen had been in the forefront of that picture.

Forgetting his wet shoes, Kellen picked up the pace and ran back to the lab. He needed to call Caine and get a copy of that newspaper.

The doctor was watching him even before he made that appointment!

Chapter 15

A half hour later Kellen was on the phone with Caine. Wearing a lab coat and a pair of old, worn sweatpants that Gabriel had stuffed in his locker, he carved out a path in front of the computer, waiting for his old boss to e-mail him the newspaper cover.

"Why did you want this again?" Caine asked. Kellen could hear the vampire typing.

"Our bombing victim had a ton of newspapers in his secret apartment. One of them was the *Necropolis Times*, with the OCU's picture on the front page. That's just too much of a coincidence for me."

"Yes, that does seem odd." More typing. "It should be coming through now."

Kellen tapped at the keyboard, opened his e-mail account and watched as the full-page spread of the newspaper filled his screen, pixel by pixel.

"Thanks, Caine."

"No problem. How are you faring in other matters?"

Kellen rubbed a hand over his head. "Everything's cool."

There was a long pause on Caine's end. Kellen knew the vampire could sense his lie. Even over the phone, the vampire could probably smell his untruth. He possessed that much power.

"Okay. Will you be coming home soon?"

Home was an alien notion for him. He had never truly felt at home anywhere.

Movement at the door forced Kellen's head up. Sophie walked into the room, her shoulders back, her chin high. She wouldn't even meet his gaze.

"I don't know," he finally said into the phone. "There are a few things I need to take care of first."

"Ah, I see. It's always about a woman, isn't it?" He sighed. "Call if you need any more help."

"Sure will." Kellen didn't say goodbye, but flipped the phone closed and set it on the computer table in front of him.

Sophie handed him some paper. "Here. Gabriel told me to give this to you."

Taking the offered paper, Kellen glanced over it. It was an in-depth report on Dr. Jonathon Bueller, including his family history.

"This is exactly what I needed. I'm surprised Gabriel knew what I was looking for. I didn't get a chance to tell him."

"I did the report."

Surprise lifted his brow. "You did?"

"I remembered something you said earlier about the doctor being the key to all of this, so digging deep into his past made sense. Plus, with him having a secret apartment, I thought maybe he had a secret identity, as well." She pointed to the first page he was holding. "If you look there, Jonathon Bueller doesn't go back very far. In fact, it looks like he didn't really exist until about the 1970s. But we know that the doctor is a few hundred years old, so I cross-referenced his birth date and his possible country of birth, considering he had an accent, and something did show up."

Kellen flipped to the second page of the report. As he skimmed the contents, his gut turned over. "He changed his name."

Sophie nodded. "Looks like he *was* living two lives."

"Frederick Brenner, born 1789, in Munich, Germany." Kellen mulled over the name in his mind. He recognized it from somewhere. Setting the papers aside, he tapped at the keyboard to bring up a military website. There was a search engine to find veterans that served in all the wars. He typed in Frederick Brenner. After a few minutes, the search pulled up a listing. Kellen's stomach lurched into his throat.

"He served in World War Two and in Vietnam."

Sophie moved up beside him and looked at the computer screen. "Did you know him?"

He shook his head. "I don't remember. Brenner is familiar, but I knew a lot of men over there."

"Did many vampires serve in the war?"

"You'd be surprised. We make pretty good soldiers. Stronger, quicker—heal faster, don't tire as easy."

"Super soldiers."

He frowned. "What did you say?"

"You're like super soldiers because of your enhancements."

Heart racing, Kellen headed out the door of the computer room. Sophie was right on his tail. "Where are you going?"

He strode down the hall to the workroom that held his replications of the two bombs. Quickly snapping on gloves, he rushed to the table and picked up the first bomb. Peering close, he examined the metal pipe close to the cap. He turned it over and over, until something piqued his interest. Just under the cap was a symbol and letter etched into the metal. A triangle with a *D* in the middle.

After setting that one down, he picked up the other, searching for the same thing. He found it right under the cap, etched into the steel. The same symbol.

"What did you find?" Sophie stood next to him peering at the bomb, excitement lighting her eyes.

"Maybe something. Maybe nothing."

"Tell me."

He set the pipes down. "The letter *D* is etched in

the metal inside a crude-looking triangle. A lot of bombers mark their creations with some kind of trademark—a symbol or initials—to claim it as their own. It's an ego thing."

"So you think this triangle and *D* are symbols?"

He nodded.

"Maybe it's the initial of his first name," she suggested.

"Could be, but I don't sense that."

"Then what?"

"Can we cross-reference the patient files with military records?"

"You think our guy served?"

"Yeah, I do." He sighed. "I'm thinking he may have been in the same ordnance company I was in during Vietnam. Delta Company." He lifted the sleeve on the lab coat to reveal a faint mark on his forearm. A tattoo that was quickly fading, the ink dissolving into his bloodstream. It was an eagle and in its talons was clutched a black triangle. In the middle was the letter *D*.

After two hours of looking through files and cross-referencing them with old military records, Kellen and Sophie managed to sift out five possible suspects; eight males and two females, and all of them were vampires who had served in either WWII or Vietnam. Kellen kept the files on the two females to the side.

Sophie cocked her brow. "Why are you tossing them out?"

"Women don't bomb."

"Why not?"

He shrugged. "Because it's not personal enough. During all the time I've been doing this, I've never met one female bomber."

"Doesn't mean it can't happen."

"No, it doesn't, but the odds are really slim." He patted the other files. "Let's concentrate on the probables first. Besides, women didn't serve in the field during Vietnam."

"Maybe either of them or both are the sister or mother or wife of someone who did."

"That's possible but highly unlikely."

"Fine, but I think you're being sexist." She swiveled in her chair, giving him her back.

The tension in the room could fill a hot air balloon and lift it to the moon. When immersed in the job, everything went smoothly. They worked with each other as if they'd been partners for years instead of just days. But the second they veered from that course, friction developed between them.

It didn't surprise him, though. He would have been concerned if he didn't feel the conflict between them. It actually would have stung his pride a bit to know that she was finding it easy to work with him despite their short history.

Looking at her back, he was about to say something, when Olena swept into the room, carrying brown bags full of takeout. The heavenly scent of chow mein floated to him.

"Anyone hungry?"

"Olena, you are an angel."

She laughed. "That's one I've never been called." She handed Kellen a bag.

He ripped it open and inhaled the delectable smell of Chinese food.

"You shouldn't thank me, anyway," she said as she tore open another bag. "Sophie ordered it."

He turned to look at Sophie. She smiled with a mouthful of noodles. "What? I was hungry for Chinese and thought everyone could use a break."

"I could kiss you right about now."

"Please don't." She dipped her head down, putting her attention back on her food, but not before he caught the blush on her cheeks.

God, he loved when she did that. He was smitten and couldn't deny it any longer. And the woman ordered him Chinese food. How could it get any better than that?

Contented, Kellen opened the lid of one Styrofoam container and dug into the chow mein with the plastic fork. Once the food hit his tongue, he was moaning with happiness.

"Mmm, man, this tastes good!"

Olena smiled around an egg roll. "I love a man who's easily pleased."

"I find that hard to believe, Olena," he chided.

Olena burst out laughing, and when Kellen turned he saw that Sophie was trying to hide her smile behind a hand. He joined in. It felt so good to share camaraderie with these two women. From the first moment he'd been introduced, it seemed like he'd been working here forever. It felt natural.

Not that he hadn't had a good working relationship with those in the OCU back in Necropolis. He had fit in until he started to change, and everything irritated him. Now he knew it was because of the *Sangcerritus,* but before being diagnosed he thought it was because none of them liked having him around. They would go out of their way to avoid him.

Here, because there was no way to hide his condition, both Olena and Sophie, even Gabriel in his own way, had accepted him for who he was. It felt good to not be feared.

"Hey, Olena, I've been meaning to ask you," he began, "Just how old are you?"

The fork heading to her mouth halted in midair as she lifted one elegant brow. "How old do you think I am?"

"At least two hundred."

Sophie snorted. "I can't believe you're talking about your age so casually. I thought it was rude to ask a lady about that."

"It's different for vampires. The older you are the more powerful you are assumed to be. For a lady, being close to three hundred is a good thing." Olena grinned.

"Well?"

"Do you know who Marie Antoinette was?"

Kellen smirked. "Of course. I saw the movie."

Sophie laughed at that. And it warmed Kellen's heart to hear it. He smiled at her, and this time she didn't turn away.

"Well, I was her governess for many years before she moved to the French courts."

Kellen nodded, impressed. "I knew you were older than me."

She waved her fork at him. "Oh, the stories I could tell you. I visited her quite often in Versailles. What fun."

"Do you miss it, Olena?" Sophie asked. By the look on her face, Kellen thought she was really asking something else.

Olena shook her head. "I've enjoyed every era I've been in. Including this one. There's something to be said about all of them." Then she looked pensive. "It's the people I've loved that I miss. Unfortunately, not everyone I had a relationship with was a vampire. But the heart is fickle, *non?*" She smiled at Sophie, then turned that same knowing look onto Kellen.

He dropped his gaze and turned his attention to his food, intently shoveling noodles into his mouth. God, that woman saw way too much. It was spooky. She had a lot in common with Caine and his ability to sense when someone was lying, or to know exactly how they were feeling. Kellen didn't want to be transparent like that. How could she know what he was feeling for Sophie, when *he* didn't really know?

He risked a glance at Sophie. Her head was down, too, avoiding Olena's raised eyebrow and that look of omnipotence. He wanted to laugh at the ridiculousness of it.

But he didn't get a chance, because Gabriel burst into the room with a none-too-pleased look on his face. "Grab your gear. There was another bombing."

Chapter 16

The bombing site was a media circus when they arrived. Television trucks and newspaper journalists, as well as curious onlookers, swarmed the area. Yellow police tape, and roadblocks, sectioned off two city streets around the central site, which was another bar. This one catered to lycans.

Unfortunately, the place wasn't empty went the bomb went off. They didn't know the exact tally of casualties, but with every minute the recovery crew dug in the rubble, the number increased. So far, they were looking at three dead and still counting.

Sophie's stomach roiled as she ducked under the tape to enter the crime scene. She'd learned to close herself off for the most part; it was difficult to do the job if emotions clouded the process. But the possibility that she might know some of the victims hit her hard.

Sucking in a breath to calm her nerves, she tightened her grip on the handle of her crime scene kit and, head up, followed Gabriel into the blasted area. She felt a comforting hand on her shoulder as she walked. Glancing over her shoulder, she saw Kellen right behind her, his eyes full of sympathy.

It unnerved her that he sensed she needed that hand of support. Was she that readable? No other man, not even her own pack alpha, could tell what she was thinking.

"You can't read my thoughts, can you?" she asked him cautiously.

He shook his head. "No, but I can read you."

Uncertain if that made her happy or scared, she nodded to him, but didn't say anything. She felt like a rookie on her first scene. There was no room for her emotions if she was going to do a thorough job. Later she could cry. But now the victims needed her to have her head on straight.

The first thing she noticed upon entering the scene was the size of the blast radius. Twice the diameter of the one at the medical center and the doctor's apartment. The bomb obviously was twice the size. Was their bomber escalating? It didn't make sense to her, especially if the initial bombs were meant for the doctor.

Kellen was next to her, surveying the damage. "It's not the same guy."

"That's what I was thinking."

Gabriel stopped and looked at him. "You can tell that right off?"

"The blast radius is too big for a simple pipe bomb. Our guy likes simplicity and uniformity. This mess," he waved his hand around at the massive destruction, "was caused by C-4 or an equivalent explosive agent."

Gabriel surveyed the area and nodded. "The superintendent thinks they're all related. Or at least he wants them to be, to make his job easier."

"He's a politician. Of course he wants it easy," Sophie added.

"Okay, let's work the scene, gather our evidence and get back to the lab to figure this one out."

"Do you think it's this NORM group?" Kellen asked.

Gabriel's face darkened and Sophie knew anger simmered just under the surface of his usually calm exterior. "Yes, I do. There are quite a few humans who work and live here. People are going to start pointing fingers soon, and we're going to have citywide panic."

The superintendent took that moment to enter the crime scene. He made a beeline toward them. "Inspector, a word please."

Gabriel nodded to the team. "Get what you can and take it back to the lab. Kellen, see if you can piece this bomb together and give us a lead to follow."

"No problem."

The inspector shoved his hands into his pockets and left with the superintendent.

Sophie, Kellen and Olena marched into the chaos to find evidence to catch a killer.

Tossing her house keys onto the kitchen counter, Sophie ran a hand through her hair, pulling it out of its usual ponytail. She shook her hair out and rubbed at her sore scalp. She had a headache and it seemed to be mounting.

The day had been long and exhausting, both physically and mentally. They had worked the scene for over five hours, and came away with bags of debris to analyze. When they returned to the lab, she announced she was going home for a couple of hours of rest. No one argued, especially since she had weeks of vacation and sick time saved up, and the fact that one of the victims had been a member of her pack. She hadn't known Cheryl well, but had associated with her at pack functions.

Kellen had looked at her but said nothing. She didn't know what she would have done if he had asked to come with her, if she needed some company. In her state, she feared she would have said yes. So she was glad that he hadn't asked. And maybe, just maybe, he had known that.

She opened the refrigerator door and searched the contents. Her stomach growled for some real food. The chow mein she had eaten earlier sat in her gut like a lump of coal.

She grabbed lettuce, tomatoes, and cucumber for a salad, and a package of steak. She needed some red meat. Maybe after her meal she'd go for a run. It had been over four days since she'd shifted and stretched out her wolf legs.

As she was putting the salad together, her doorbell rang. Her heart thumped in her chest. Had Kellen followed her home? Her palms started to sweat at the prospect. She had to admit she wouldn't be upset if he had. In a way, she would have been flattered that despite her protestations, he chose to come anyway.

Wiping her hands on her jeans, she smoothed a hand over her hair and moved toward the door, anticipation rushing through her veins. She wrapped her hand over the knob, twisted, and pulled the door open. Disappointment roared over her in a blast of cool wind. She should have smelled her father coming up the porch steps.

"Leon?"

"Hello, Sophie. Can I come in?"

"Of course." She fully opened the door to her pack alpha. A lycan always opened her door to her alpha, no matter what. If he came here to her home, it was important. The last time Leon had been in her house was over seven months ago. That time was to tell her that her brother, Gaston, was getting married.

Leon removed his shoes then came into her living

room and made himself comfortable on her sofa. Nervously, she did a quick survey of her place to make sure nothing was out of the ordinary, that she didn't have anything embarrassing lying around that he might see and comment on.

"Would you like a drink?"

"No, nothing, thank you, Sophie. I just came to talk."

She swallowed around the lump in her throat and sat on the sofa beside him.

"You had a hard day." It wasn't a question. Leon would have known immediately that Cheryl had been one of the victims of the bombing. Most pack lycans had their alpha listed as a next of kin.

"So have you. It must be hard to lose a member of the pack."

He nodded. "Yes. It's the hardest in circumstances like these. Do you have any leads into who did the bombing?"

"Not yet, but we will."

"I know you will." He reached across the back of the sofa and patted her hand that rested there. "You're a good investigator."

She gave him a little smile, unaccustomed to his compliments.

"So I hear you have someone…else working the case."

Ah, there was the real reason he had come knocking on her door. Pulling her hand out from under his, Sophie stood. "Did Duncan talk to you?"

"He's concerned about your interaction with this person."

"His name is Kellen."

Leon waved his hand like he was batting away a bad smell. "Is there something going on between you and this vampire, this Kellen?"

Wrapping her arms around her body, she turned from him, not wanting him to see her face as she lied. "No. And Duncan should mind his own business."

"You are his business, Sophie."

She wheeled around and pointed her finger. "He's your business, Leon. I told you I'd go on one date with him, and I did. That doesn't mean that I'm going to mate with him. I don't care if he's your right hand. He's a Neanderthal."

"And this vampire is not?"

"No, he isn't, if you have to know. He's actually one of the most intelligent, charming men I've ever met."

"He's a vampire, Sophie, and from what I've heard, not a very stable one at that."

"Is this why you are here, Alpha? To warn me away from Kellen. To threaten me with some terrible fate if I decide I want to have a relationship with the vampire."

"No, I'm here as your *father,* to ask you to think about what your relationship with this vampire could do to your pack and to your family. I can't believe you don't remember the upheaval the last one brought to you."

She shook her head. "It's just like you to bring up the father card when nothing else is working."

"And it's just like my daughter to fight me on every-thing."

"Well, I wouldn't want to disappoint you."

He sighed and rubbed a hand over his haggard face.

The years hadn't been kind to her father. Years of running the pack had taken its toll on him. He looked old and beaten. Or it could have been that he only looked that way when he was arguing with her. Over the years, she'd made a habit of it.

It wasn't easy being the alpha's daughter. Every young lycan had an eye on her while she was growing up. And every one of them desired her for different reasons. Most for what she could do for their aspirations to be alpha. Her brother, Gaston, had the first right to the job, but another male wolf could challenge him. Now, if that particular man had *her* on his arm, it would go a long way to winning popularity among the pack. Their pack was a democracy, and the best man was voted in. Not like in the old days, when lycans fought to the death for the right to lead. Blood battle had been abolished thirty years ago. But it *was* how Leon had won his place.

"You don't disappoint me, Sophie. But you haven't always done what's best for the pack."

"That's your job, Leon, not mine. I'm not the alpha and never will be."

He shook his head again. "So stubborn and rebelli-ous. I don't know where you get it."

"Mom, probably." Because of the hurt look in his

eyes, Sophie was almost sorry for mentioning her mother. When Sophie had been only thirteen, her mother, Elsa, left the pack and went on tour with her musician friend, who just happened to be a vampire. Even though Elsa had been the alpha's mate, she had been shunned by the pack for her behavior.

Leon had been devastated. But he hid it for the sake of the pack and for his children. But she knew how much it hurt him, not only because he had loved her so much, but because it made him look weak as an Alpha.

Elsa returned to the pack eight months later, after Leon had tracked her and brought her back, but it hadn't been the same between them. Or with Sophie. She tried to visit with her mom at least once a week, but it was difficult to see her. She looked so broken and sad, like a huge piece of her had been ripped out.

She knew she was being childish by bringing it up and by arguing with him like this, but sometimes she couldn't help it. He was her father, but he hadn't always been there for her. The welfare of the pack had always been more important than her needs. And sometimes those two things were in direct competition.

Like now.

"I didn't come here to argue with you, Sophie. I came here concerned for you. To make sure that you weren't making a big mistake."

"Well, I'm not. You don't have to worry about it. It's been all taken care of. Kellen and I don't have a relationship and don't plan on having one."

He stood and moved toward her. He lifted his arms up to hug her, but when she didn't advance toward him, he patted her shoulder instead. "I'm glad we had this talk. Everything will work out for the best. You'll see."

She nodded, not trusting herself to speak. If she formed the words she wanted, she knew her father would never forgive her. No matter their differences over the years, she wasn't quite sure she could live with that. She wasn't sure she was ready to give up the sanctity and safety of the pack, or the promise of a big family one day, for one man, no matter how amazing he may be or how incredible he made her feel.

"I'll see you at the meeting later this month." Leaning down, he pressed a quick kiss on her cheek, patted her shoulder again and after slipping on his shoes, promptly left.

Angry but conflicted, Sophie stomped back into the kitchen to eat. Her stomach was beyond rumbling. When she was upset she liked to eat meat, the bloodier the better.

Ripping open the plastic covering the steak, she grabbed the meat in her hand and tore at it. She was too upset to cook the damn thing, or waste her time cutting it into small pieces. It always tasted better this way anyway.

As she ate she thought about Kellen. What she wouldn't give to see him right now. To snuggle into his warmth and take comfort from the way he touched and kissed her. He made her feel extraordinary. Worthwhile, and not because she was the alpha's daughter. She knew

he didn't give a damn about any of that political nonsense. He wanted her. For her.

And that made a difference in her world. But was it
enough to risk everything her life was based on?

Her mother had sacrificed everything for eight
months of pleasure, but was she really willing to do the
same? Sure, her father had taken her back when most
in the pack called for her banishment. Would he make
the same concessions for her? She didn't know—and
she wasn't sure she really wanted to find out.

Chapter 17

The water pooling in the huge frond leaf overhead dripped down onto the brim of Kellen's helmet.

It was raining again in Vietnam.

When didn't it rain? It was the soggiest country he'd ever been to. Which was saying a lot, since he'd traveled to many places in the past eighty years.

Kellen wiped at the moisture beading on his forehead before it dribbled into his eyes and impeded his vision. Although he had superior eyesight even in the night, the claustrophobic dark of the jungle nearly suffocated him into inaction.

Sometimes he just wished he could sit in a tall tree overlooking everything and everyone and wait out this stupid war. To think he had even enlisted for this job.

"Psst, Falcon. Wake up, man, and hand me that charge."

Startled from his crouch along the trail, Kellen handed a claymore mine to his squad sergeant.

The sergeant shoved the two prongs into the ground, underneath thick foliage, unrolled the detonator wire from it and then walked it in a squat across the trail to where Kellen was crouching. They would unravel the wire until they reached their position fifty yards away, where they would detonate the explosive when needed. It was the tenth booby trap they'd set in the past four hours.

Two platoons from Delta company were hunkered down about two miles from their position, preparing to mount an offensive against a group of Viet Cong that had retreated into a nearby village. Kellen and the sergeant were ensuring that any of those who escaped the village wouldn't get away.

When Kellen had enlisted, he supposed he did it so he could blow stuff up, but what he didn't realize was that most of the stuff he was going to blow up in Vietnam was going to be people.

He had three months to go on his tour of duty. Once he got out, he made an oath that he'd never get involved in another war. Vampire or not, the last place he wanted to end his days was on a battlefield. Being blown up by a grenade would kill him, just like it would anyone else in his platoon.

During his ten months in-country he ran into twenty

other vampires. Five of them were in his company but none in his own ordnance platoon. He had heard the news recently of a vampire in another platoon getting blown up by his own explosive. He didn't want to die like that.

The sergeant tapped Kellen's helmet, indicating he was ready to move out.

Kellen slung his M-16 over his shoulder and duck-walked behind the sergeant as he made his way toward their designated position.

But they didn't get very far before rapid-fire gunshots echoed through the dense clumping of trees and bushes.

Halting, his sergeant pointed toward an overgrown section of brush, then crawled, belly to the ground, over the dirt path and into it. Kellen followed his lead. Setting up position on his stomach, Kellen wiped his eye clear and peered through the scope, waiting for the enemy to appear.

More gunfire sounded, this time closer. Kellen could also hear the shouts of both the Americans and the Viet Cong. To his dismay, the battle had started early.

Breath coming in slow easy draws, Kellen waited, peering through the scope for any sign of the Viet Cong. The moment he spotted any, he'd let the sarge know, so he could detonate the claymores.

Sweat dripped into his eyes as he waited, and he wiped at it with the back of his hand. All the sounds around him were louder in his ears. He could hear the sergeant's quick heartbeat, racing like a hummingbird's wings. He could hear the raindrops splattering on the leaves and in the dirt. It sounded like tin drums.

Ping.

Ping.

Ping.

Then he heard the approach of footsteps down the now muddy trail. But he didn't think it was a man approaching.

Blinking to clear his vision, he watched in surprise as an animal padded out of the thick jungle. A wolf ran toward him, its eyes glowing like blue fire, its beautiful auburn coat wet with rain.

She was spectacular.

Jumping to his feet, Kellen lifted his gun and started out onto the trail toward her. He had to get to her before the enemy did.

His sergeant called after him, but Kellen didn't slow. There was no time. It was slipping away even as he moved. His legs were starting to feel leaden, as if he was running through a viscous liquid pool.

More gunfire sounded. The echoes bounced off the nearby trees. The enemy was close. She would get hurt.

Trying to run faster, Kellen reached out toward the beast. If he could reach her, he could protect her with his body.

The enemy appeared from the bushes nearby, rifles pointing in the wolf's direction.

"Sophie!" he screamed.

Kellen jumped and wrapped his body around the animal, taking them both to the ground. He hit solidly, his breath shoved from his lungs.

A sharp pain rushed up his spine. He'd been shot.

"Kellen?"

Was it her voice? Was the wolf speaking to him?

"Wake up."

A pressure on his shoulder jerked him awake. Sitting up, Kellen glanced around and tried to get his balance. He felt dizzy and confused. He'd only been asleep for a few minutes, hadn't he?

Blinking, he focused on the woman standing in front of him, a look of concern on her elegant pale face. "Sophie?"

"Yeah." She frowned.

"I thought you went home for a few hours."

"I did. It's six in the morning."

"Oh."

"Are you okay? You were twitching in your sleep."

Mortified, he hoped he hadn't called out her name while asleep. He wondered how long she'd been watching him.

"Did I say anything?"

She shook her head but looked at him strangely. Was she lying and not just telling him, so he wouldn't be embarrassed? Or maybe it was her embarrassment she was hiding, that her name had been upon his lips while he was asleep.

Somewhat relieved, he nodded and rubbed a hand over his mouth, self-conscious. He'd been asleep sitting up, head and arms over the desk. Not the most comfortable way to sleep, and certainly not the most flattering, either.

"I guess I was more tired than I thought." He twisted side to side trying to get out the kinks that had settled into his spine.

She pointed to her forehead. "Umm, you have a Post-it note stuck."

Reaching up, he pulled a square piece of yellow paper from his head. He'd fallen asleep making notes about the various files. "Thanks." He stuck the note back onto a file folder—where he had previously fastened it.

"What was the dream about?"

"Vietnam."

She moved closer to him, her hands stuffed into her pants pockets. He wondered if she had them there to stop her from breaching the distance between them and touching him. She looked like that was what she wanted to do. Instead, she asked, "Was it bad? You look paler than normal."

Nodding, he stood and stretched out his legs. "Bad enough."

She kept his gaze as if she wanted to say something to him. But after taking in a deep breath, she turned her attention to the desk where the files were spread out in disarray. She tapped her finger on one of them. "Did you come up with anything?"

"Yeah." He dragged two file folders toward him and

flipped them open. "Both these guys were patients, one present, one past, and they both served in Vietnam from 1966 to 1968 during the time Brenner was there."

"Was that the time you were there?"

"Yeah."

"Do you recognize either of them?"

He shook his head as he stared down at the photos of the two men. "Not right out. This name might be familiar," he said, pointing to the file on one Louis Martin, "but I can't be definite. I've known quite a few Louises in my lifetime."

"Any of the surveillance photos match?"

He pulled two eight-by-ten glossy pictures across the desk and set them in front of Sophie. She eyed them, then the photos from the files. She nodded. "Could be either of them. They have similar builds and the same color hair."

"Yeah, but only Jacques DuPont had an appointment that afternoon."

"Did you call Gabriel?"

"Twice. He never called me back."

"Why didn't you call me?"

He shrugged. "You didn't give me your number."

"Oh, right." She gathered the files together, fidgeting with the top flap.

He could tell there was something on her mind, something she wanted to say to him. He moved closer to her, but not so close that she would feel pressured.

"You were in my dream."

She looked at him, her eyes narrowed. "Just now? The one about the war?"

He nodded. His throat felt dry, like leather out in the sun too long. Her presence in his dream scared him. He normally wasn't one for premonitions, but this one had needled at his mind like one. It could have been just his fear for her safety. But he couldn't shake the sensation that it was more, so much more than that.

"Promise me you'll be careful."

Her nose scrunched up. "What do you mean?"

"Just be careful, okay?" He sighed, grasping her hand in his and running his thumb over her knuckles. "Don't take any unnecessary risks on this one."

"Do you have visions?"

He shook his head. "No, just a feeling."

"Look, I've been on the job for years. Every case has a certain amount of risk." She slowly pulled her hand from his and tucked it into her pocket. "Besides that, I can take care of myself. I'm a lycan, after all."

He went to say something else, to tell her he was afraid of losing her, but Gabriel took that unwelcome moment to march into the room.

"Sorry I didn't get back to you."

Sophie showed him the files. "Kellen found us a couple of prime suspects."

Briefly glancing down at the names and addresses, Gabriel flipped open his cell phone. He nodded to Kellen. "Good job. We'll get backup to meet us at the DuPont address."

Kellen nodded, but his heart wasn't into it. He was happy that he was able to put some of the pieces together on this case, but something about it was nagging him. He had a feeling that digging deeper was only going to get someone hurt. And he feared that someone might be Sophie.

Chapter 18

Jacques DuPont's apartment was downtown, in a fashionable part of the city. Winding cobblestone streets lined with quaint cafes and designer boutiques meshed with the best in nightlife clubbing.

Kellen sat in the backseat of Gabriel's Audi as he and a special police task force amassed on the apartment building's front stoop and at the back, in the alley. He and Sophie were told to wait in the vehicle until they cleared the man's apartment and hopefully had him in custody so they could question him about the black briefcase he was photographed carrying into the medical center the day Dr. Bueller's office exploded.

Kellen didn't mind sitting in the vehicle. He was

never one for police action. Unlike some crime scene investigators he knew, he didn't get into the field because he wanted to be a cop or thought it would be a good stepping-stone onto the force. No, he liked working in the lab, where he could assemble together all the puzzle pieces. Behind the scenes was always better than being out in the open, in the line of fire. He'd been in the line of fire before and he hated it.

He stole a glance at Sophie as she sat staring out the window from the front seat. From her tensed shoulders, he guessed she hated being out of the action. He smiled to himself, thinking she probably loved the thrill of the chase. It had to have been a lycan thing for sure. Most of the best cops he knew were lycans.

Suddenly she perked up and pointed to something out on the street. "Isn't that him?"

Kellen followed her line of vision to see a dark-haired man with an average build sauntering down the street. As he neared the building, his gait slowed until, finally, he stopped and stared at the front door, where several officers and Gabriel were entering.

Looking around him, he turned and went back the way he had come from. Quickly.

"Yeah, that's him."

Sophie was out of the car before Kellen finished his sentence.

"Sophie!" Kellen pulled at the door handle and jumped out of the vehicle as Sophie crossed the street in pursuit of the suspect. He jogged to catch up to her.

Once at her side, he glanced at her. "What's your plan? Run this guy down?"

"Something like that."

"All right. I got your back."

Sophie didn't have time to respond, because their suspect, Jacques, had made them and was upping his pace by dashing across the street and turning the corner. She took off first, Kellen following behind. She was fast, and he had to make a real effort to keep up to her.

Jacques was sprinting hard, weaving back and forth down the sidewalk to avoid colliding with people. Sophie was now only about three yards behind him, and Kellen about two feet behind her.

As he ran, Kellen thanked the clouds above that the sun wasn't beating down on him. He wouldn't have lasted long, baking in the ultraviolet rays, but then neither would their suspect.

Jacques turned another corner, making a wide berth around a woman and her baby carriage. Sophie barreled right toward them, crouching for a second, then leaping about six feet in the air and landing safely on the other side, without breaking stride.

Kellen nearly ran into the stroller as he watched Sophie glide through the air. At the last moment, he made an arc around them and continued the chase. Now Sophie was about seven feet in front of him and gaining on the suspect.

The street they had turned onto was a wide board-walk lined with majestic trees, but it was crowded with people milling about at various kiosks, shopping or hawking wares, and scenic cafes selling iced cappuccinos, red wine and atmosphere. One cafe had its tables scattered across the pavement, and a line of scooters and Vespas crowded around them. Someone was going to get hurt in that mess.

Kellen watched as Jacques jumped over empty chairs and tried to weave around patrons, but to no avail, a few people went flying into the street as he collided with them.

"Move out of the way!" Sophie yelled as she waved her hands at the crowd.

Some did move, but most heard her warning too late. Kellen cringed as Sophie came sprinting through the cafe, knocking tables and scooters over as she ran. Kellen followed the path she cleared.

Jacques weaved across the street, stopping traffic as he went, and nearly getting hit by a large garbage truck. It screeched to a stop about half a foot away. Sophie followed him, much more agile and quick. She jumped over one car and slid across the hood of another.

Kellen followed her across the road, but without as much style. Hand out, he avoided the cars as much as possible. But one motorcycle skidded to a halt too late and nicked him in the knee. Pain ripped through him, but he didn't stop. Nothing was broken. He'd heal.

Sophie glanced back at him and looked as if she was going to slow. But he shook his head at her. "Keep going!"

Whipping her head back around she kept on running. Kellen followed, realizing that he was falling behind. He thought he was in good shape, but compared to Sophie he was an amateur.

Chasing Jacques around another corner, Kellen saw a huge obstacle in the way. A large stone fountain with a circular pond encasing it sat in the middle of the walkway. The way Jacques was going, he looked as though he was going to run right into it.

At the last second, he dodged around it. This gave Sophie her opportunity, if Kellen was right about what she planned to do. Sprinting straight at the stone structure, Sophie leapt onto the edge of the pond, pushed off with her back foot and sailed over the fountain, her feet churning in the air to give her continual motion.

As she landed on the other side, Kellen lost sight of her.

Pushing harder until his lungs burned, he wheeled around the fountain, but came to a screeching halt when he saw Sophie on the ground, cradling her ankle.

A few people had crowded around her, asking her if she was all right.

He pushed past them and crouched beside her. Tears rolled down her cheeks. Between her fingers he could see blood and bone. Her ankle bone had punctured her skin.

He brushed at the tendrils of hair sticking to her sweaty brow. "I'm calling Gabriel." He flipped open his cell phone.

"Keep going," she grunted between clenched teeth. "Don't let him get away."

"I won't leave you."

"I'll be okay. I'll heal. It just hurts like hell right now." She grabbed onto his arm. "Go. Take him down."

A siren wailed in the background. Someone had obviously already called an ambulance.

Looking down at her, he saw the disappointment in her eyes. He didn't want to let her down. He wanted to be a hero for her.

Pressing a kiss to her forehead, he murmured, "I'll be back." She nodded, her face pale and sweaty.

Standing, Kellen surveyed the street and saw the tail end of Jacques's green shirt as he dashed down a one-way street.

Kellen ran after him, the defeated look on Sophie's face propelling him forward.

After two more blocks, Kellen lost Jacques. He had darted down a narrow lane leading to a dead end, and then Kellen had lost sight of him. There was really nowhere Jacques could have gone, but it looked as if the man had disappeared anyway.

Maybe the vampire could mist. In Kellen's long lifetime, he'd only encountered one vampire who possessed that ability. To dissolve into nothing and reassemble elsewhere like a floating mist. He really hoped Jacques didn't possess that kind of anomaly.

Vigilant, Kellen slowed his pace and crept along the road, his gaze eyeing the surrounding nooks and crannies in the old stone buildings. Jacques had to have gone somewhere; inside one of the buildings, maybe.

As he walked, he noticed a fire escape along one building. A perfect way to disappear. When he neared it, Kellen noticed a group of four teens milling about on the steps of one of the apartment buildings across the street. If Jacques went up they would have had to have seen him.

Jogging across the road, Kellen approached them. One of the boys noticed him and nudged the others. They all began to act as if they didn't have a care in the world, except about how cool they were. Little did they know that Kellen had invented that attitude about one hundred and eighty years ago. And since not one of them was a vampire, they couldn't say the same.

"Hey, how long have you been here?"

They all did the collective shrug, but one of them, obviously the mouth of the group, answered, "Why do you want to know?"

"Because a friend of mine came this way and I need to know where he went." He glanced at each of them. None of them met his gaze. "He has dark hair, average build and is wearing a green shirt."

"What are you, a cop or something?" the only female in the group asked.

"Or something."

"If we give you that info, what are you going to give us?"

Leaning toward them, Kellen put on the power and

bared his fangs. He knew his eyes were glowing, and likely other energy was flowing from him. They all shrank back.

"I'll let you keep your lives." He licked the tips of his fangs. "I've been running for ten blocks now and I'm awfully thirsty."

"You can't do that," the mouth stuttered. "It's illegal to take blood out on the street, dude."

"Hey, I'm from out of town, 'dude.' I'll take blood wherever I choose to."

One by one, they pointed to the fire escape. The girl said, "He went up there. To the roof."

"Thanks." Kellen dug out the cell phone from his pants pocket and flipped it open. He dialed Gabriel's number. The inspector answered on the first ring.

"Where are you?"

Kellen glanced around. "I don't know, hold on." He glanced at the teens. "Where am I?"

One of the boys rattled off the address.

"I'm on Jardin and Trois Rivières. The suspect is on the roof."

"Two units are on their way."

"How is Sophie?"

"She's okay and is on her way to the hospital."

Kellen crossed the street toward the fire escape. "Good. I'll see you soon." He snapped the phone closed and slid it into his pocket.

Reaching to grab the end of the metal ladder, Kellen pulled himself up and swung a leg high, hooking the bottom rung. After mounting the first step, the rest was a piece of cake, and Kellen was up the fire escape in a matter of seconds.

Once on the roof, he scanned the area. There weren't very many obstacles to hide behind, but on first glance he couldn't see the suspect anywhere. Walking across the pebbled roof, he swung his gaze from left to right, in case Jacques decided to jump out at him.

Halfway across, the roof door burst open and two constables charged out onto the roof, guns raised.

The lead constable was Duncan Quinn.

"Police! Get on your knees!"

Kellen put his hands up in defense. "Whoa! It's me, Duncan."

The lycan never flinched. "I said get on your knees and put your hands on your head."

Kellen stopped moving and met Duncan's gaze. "You know damn well who I am, Duncan. Don't be stupid."

The other officer glanced nervously at Duncan, then back to Kellen. He lowered his weapon.

Gun still pointed, Duncan glared at Kellen. He could see the rage in the lycan's eyes, and knew he'd have no qualms about shooting Kellen where he stood, no questions asked.

The tension in the air was thick. Kellen tried not to flinch, or even breathe. He knew Duncan was just itching for an excuse, any excuse, to pull the trigger.

Thankfully, Jacques had the presence of mind to pop out of his hiding spot, with his hands up. "I surrender. I surrender."

The other officer swiveled around and raised his weapon toward Jacques. "Come out—nice and slow."

Jacques did exactly as he was told. He walked out partway, went to his knees, and hooked his hands behind his head. The other constable came around behind him and handcuffed him.

Duncan still hadn't moved.

With the suspect in custody, the other officer approached Duncan. "We got the suspect, Quinn. You can holster your weapon."

Eyes still blazing with hate, Duncan slowly lowered his gun and holstered it. Once he had snapped it closed, only then did he lower his gaze. "We're not even close to being even, vampire."

Turning, he followed his partner through the open door.

Once he was gone, Kellen let out the breath he was holding. Sweat soaked the back of his shirt. He'd stared down many a weapon in his life, but this was the first time he actually thought he might die. It was a sobering thought. And one he didn't want to dwell on.

But it reminded him that he didn't have much time left. The disease was still rushing through him, bombarding his brain. Sooner or later it would end him.

He just hoped it was later, much later, so he could spend as much time as he could with Sophie. She was the only thing in his life that made him feel like he had something to live for.

Chapter 19

After watching four hours of interrogation by the inspector, it was evident to Kellen that Jacques DuPont
was not their bomber.

The guy had other problems. Major issues for which
he would likely see the inside of a jail cell, but he wasn't
blowing things up. He'd served in Vietnam, but in
supply. It was obvious now what the guy had been sup-
plying.

He was a drug dealer, selling Vampatimine, an
ecstasy-like drug manufactured from vampire saliva,
out on the street to anyone that wanted it.

The police had found his secret stash, and a false
backing in his closet had led to a small lab to make the

drug. His drug had also been linked to several date rapes that had been recorded over the past year. All in all, it was a good arrest that would hopefully solve a few open cases.

Which left them with one name and address to still check out—Louis Martin.

The moment Gabriel came out of the interrogation room, Kellen pounced on him. "Let's check out the other address."

"A team is already there. I called them out the second I realized that DuPont wasn't our man." He started down the hallway back to his office.

Kellen kept pace. "Have you heard anything?"

"No. But I should any minute." Just as predicted, Gabriel's cell phone shrilled. He answered it.

After a few cursory nods and okays, he flipped the phone shut. "Louis wasn't home. They're searching the house now."

"Maybe we should go over there."

They reached Gabriel's office. "And maybe you should go and take a break. Get something to eat and get some sleep. You look like you could use it."

Kellen nodded, thinking it over. "Is Sophie still at the hospital?"

"She's at home, resting. But I don't think that's the best place for you, do you?"

Kellen kept the inspector's gaze. He knew what he was saying to him, but Kellen was a stubborn man. "I like her, Gabriel."

"I know."

"And I believe she likes me back."

"I know that, too." He put his hand on Kellen's shoulder. "Pack politics are complicated, Kellen. You have to know that. Just as there are rules in the vampire society, in Nouveau Monde there are rules in the lycan one, too."

"I'm not big on rules," Kellen muttered.

Gabriel snorted. "I've noticed."

"Are you warning me away from her, Gabriel?" There was a tinge of menace in his voice that he couldn't keep out. He was getting tired of being told who he couldn't have a relationship with.

"No, just giving you some friendly advice." He let his hand slide off of Kellen's shoulder. "I'm not your keeper, or Sophie's, but I am her boss and her friend. I will be rather upset if she gets hurt."

"Why does everyone assume I'm going to hurt her?"

"Because it can't work between you two. You know it as well as I do." He narrowed his eyes and regarded Kellen. "Take a break, go get some food, have a drink and relax. I'll call you if they find anything worthwhile at Louis's house." Gabriel stepped into his office and closed the door, leaving Kellen standing in the hallway alone.

Biting back the urge to slam his fist into the inspector's door, Kellen marched down the hallway and out of the building. The fresh, tantalizing night air cooled Kellen's temper somewhat. He took in a few deep breaths and forced his anger back down.

He hated to hear it, but Gabriel had been right. A relationship between Kellen and Sophie was impossible. But it didn't stop him from wanting one.

And right now he wanted to see her, to make sure she was okay. The sight of her blood and broken bone had knocked the breath from his lungs, and he was still recovering from the blow.

Hailing a taxi, Kellen instructed the driver to take him to his hotel. After a shower, a change of clothes and something to eat, maybe he'd start to feel normal again. There was a hunger deep down inside, a gnawing throb that he ached to fill. The funny thing was, he didn't think it had anything to do with food.

A rare filet mignon and a glass of red wine later, Kellen was feeling less pain.

Situated just a couple of blocks from his hotel, the restaurant he chose boasted a spectacular menu and titillating atmosphere. Both had been no empty boast. The food had been delectable and the ambiance enticing.

Catering to mostly vampires, the restaurant was dark, moody and had warm blood on tap, provided by eager human donors dressed in next to nothing. Feeling the way he was, Kellen probably could have done without the extra enticement. His nerves were already running hot; he didn't need anything, or anyone, rubbing against them.

Temptation swirled in his gut as a lovely woman

with long, silky red hair sat at his table and offered him her wrist. He thought long and hard about it. Succumbing to his desire with this substitute just might ease his hunger and dampen his need to see Sophie.

Grabbing her arm, he brought it to his nose. But when he inhaled the young human's scent and didn't detect the bold earthiness of nature, the tinge of ferocity that always clung to Sophie's skin, he lost his appetite.

Standing, he tossed his napkin on the table and bowed to the young woman. "I'm sorry, you're just not my type."

Bursting out of the restaurant door and into the balmy night, Kellen tried to shake off the feeling of unrequited desire. Although he already ate, his hunger was growing.

He tucked his hands into his leather jacket and, head down, he started to walk. He needed to expend the energy and heat swirling through him like a minitornado. Standing still to allow his thoughts to dominate him would do him no good. He'd do something stupid, that was a given.

As he strode down the sidewalk, images of Sophie tried to overtake him. Thoughts of her naked and in his arms pummeled at his brain like a ball-peen hammer. He glanced up and saw a flashing neon sign advertising just what he was looking for—a distraction. Crimson Road was just the type of club he needed— loud, raucous, and packed with interesting diversions.

The smell of sweat, alcohol and sex overtook him the moment he opened the door and made his way down the steep stairs. Lit only by flickering lamps imbedded into the brick walls, the atmosphere of the place made him nostalgic for the good old days of being a vampire. Sometimes he longed for the stylistic old crypts of New Orleans, with its haunting parish homes to stalk through like a predator. Seducing virginal women had been one of his favorite pastimes when he'd been a young vampire, still hyped on the fact that he would live for a very long time and would never age—and the fact that women seemed to find him alluring. He had loved that part.

Loud, thrashing metal blasted his ears. He reveled in the way the bass rumbled over his skin, making his hair stand at attention. Taking in a deep breath of Otherworlder frivolity, Kellen made his way to the bar and ordered scotch, neat. Slamming it back, he ordered another, and then turned to lean on the bar and check out the action.

It didn't take long to be noticed. Even in a place, like this, that catered to vampires and Goth-fixated humans who liked to revel in the darkness, Kellen stood out. A trio of attractive ladies approached him, two vampires and a human, all obviously in tune with the dangerous vibes he transmitted.

"Looking for a party?" the raven-haired vampiress purred.

The other vampiress, a striking blonde, snuggled up next to him. That left the human. She stood in front of him, not as confident, not as eager for obvious reasons, and smiled at him flirtatiously. She possessed a vulnerability that he liked and craved, which is why he turned to the blonde, grabbed her hand and pulled her toward the nearest exit. Taking the human would've been a huge mistake. He wouldn't have been able to control himself. And he didn't want to go over a line he knew he'd regret for the rest of his life.

He heard the twin sighs of regret from the ladies he left behind as he maneuvered through the crowd, the blonde in tow. He located the exit, and pushed through the door and up the stairs toward another door leading outside. Once up the stairs, he kicked that door open, dragging the vampiress with him into the alley behind the club.

She gave a feral-like growl as he backed her up onto the brick wall and nuzzled his face into her neck. Her scent, one of oranges and spice, was arousing. He wasn't sure what he wanted from her, but he needed something, anything, to combat the gnawing hunger eating him away inside.

Aggressive, like an animal, she ran her hands over him, then flipped him around so his back was to the wall. Then she went down to her knees, and starting at his ankles, ran her face over his clothes, taking in his scent and his power.

His body was shaking with need by the time she reached his neck and then his mouth. Grabbing her around the arms, Kellen yanked her close, eager to sink his teeth into her sweet, delectable vein.

"Sophie," he murmured.

The vampiress pushed out of his embrace. "Who is this Sophie?"

Groaning, Kellen leaned his back against the wall. "No one. What does it matter?"

She put her hand on her hip and regarded him from head to toe. "I think she *is* someone. Your eyes definitely aren't glowing for my sake."

He shook his head, trying to clear his thoughts. She was right. He'd been dreaming of Sophie, wishing it was her hands on him, her face nuzzling at his neck.

"I apologize." It was impolite to engage a vampire if there was no intent to follow through.

She nodded curtly, accepting his meager apology, and then marched down the alley, to go back around the main entrance and return to the club to seek another's affections.

Pushing off the wall, hands curled tight into fists, he decided he would do the same.

A half hour later, he stood on Sophie's doorstep, his hand fisted to knock on the door, but he let it fall to his side. He was making a mistake. His head screamed at him to walk away, but his heart and his soul told him to stay, to see what could happen.

Closing his eyes, he sighed and rested his forehead against the wood door. He didn't know what to do.

Chapter 20

The battered copy of *People Weekly* slid across the coffee table and landed on the carpet on the opposite side, where Sophie tossed it. Boredom was starting to grate on her. She hated sitting at home not able to be at the lab working on the case. She felt useless.

Pushing up with her arms, she repositioned herself on the sofa. Her ankle throbbed, but it was a good pain, a healing pain. Lycans were quick healers, and she was doubly so. Her father had told her it was because her blood inside was as stubborn as she was on the outside. After the first time she healed a laceration on her forearm in one day, she believed him.

It would take more than twenty-four hours to heal

her ankle, though. She'd managed to snap a bone and lacerate her skin. The skin was almost knitted back together; it was the bone that would take the most time. If she hadn't been so eager to show off her leaping skills, she wouldn't have pushed herself over the limit and landed so awkwardly.

At least they had gotten the suspect. Gabriel had phoned her to let her know and to tell her that he wasn't the guy, but that he had been a criminal, nonetheless. So that was something. To Sophie, every criminal they managed to get off the street was a just reward. Someone's daughter, mother, sister or friend would be spared the horror of being raped using Vampatamine because she and Kellen had chased down the suspect.

When the inspector called, she had asked after Kellen. Regrettably, she had heard the desperation in her own voice, and she was positive that Gabriel had heard it, too. He had promptly told her to not worry about him and heal herself. She had heard the unspoken meaning, loud and clear.

She wondered if there was anyone out there who didn't object to whether she and Kellen liked each other. It seemed as though they were coming under fire from all directions.

Not that it mattered anymore. It was obvious to them both that a relationship was next to impossible for various reasons. They would just work together and try to ignore the simmering of energy forever humming between them.

Yeah right. Good luck with that.

Pushing to a stand, Sophie hopped across the living room toward the kitchen. She needed more to eat. Fuel for healing. Right before she entered, she paused and sniffed at the air. A sweet odor wafted to her nose. It smelled like cookies, the kind she used to devour as a child. Lifting her nose, she inhaled again. It was coming from her front door.

And it smelled like cinnamon.

Hobbling across the room, she stood in front of her door, too nervous to open it. She grasped the handle, turned it and slowly pulled the heavy oak door open.

Kellen stood on her porch, his hand curled in midair, as if poised to knock, his other hand was behind his back. "I thought you'd never open the door." His voice was so wistful it made her heart throb.

"But you didn't knock."

"I know. I've been standing out here for the past half hour hoping you'd sense I wanted to."

Shaking her head, she couldn't stop her lips from curling into a smile. "Do you want to come in?"

"Yes."

She smelled the alcohol on him as she held the door open and stepped to the side to allow him entrance. Smiling, he came in, immediately surveying the living room. Once he toed off his shoes, he swung around and offered her the flowers clutched in his hidden hand.

She gazed at the roses, two red, two yellow and two pink, then noticed the torn stems. She took them and inhaled the pleasant aroma, smiling at him from over top the open buds. "They're lovely. Thank you."

"Your neighbor has a beautiful garden," he said as he wandered through the living room eyeing various pictures on the walls and knickknacks on the shelves.

"I'm not even going to ask."

He grinned. "That's probably best."

It didn't surprise her in the least that he'd stolen them from her neighbor. She actually found the action endearing and a little quirky. Smiling, she moved into the kitchen to grab a vase for the flowers.

When she returned, Kellen was sitting on the sofa, thumbing through her discarded magazine. Was he nervous for some reason? His gaze rested on everything in the room except her.

She set the flowers on the coffee table and settled in beside him.

He set the magazine on the table. "How's the ankle?"

"It's healing. It should be good as new in about a week."

"Wow, that's quick." He lifted the hand that Duncan had torn open. It was still pink with newly grown skin. "I wish I could heal that fast."

"My father says it's because I'm so stubborn."

After lowering his hand, Kellen looked at her. "Your father's your alpha, isn't he?"

"Yes. How did you know?"

"Olena told me. That must've been difficult growing up."

"Are you kidding?" she grimaced. "It's still difficult, especially now." She met his gaze, letting him know exactly what she was talking about.

He nodded. "I suppose coming here was a bad idea, huh?" Turning his head, he grinned at her and her stomach flipped over. Damn, the man could turn on the charm when he wanted to.

"Maybe a little."

That made his grin widen. "Only a little?"

She opened her mouth to respond, but before she could utter any words, Kellen gathered her in his arms and kissed her. Then he broke away, pushed her back and ran a shaky hand over his face.

"I'm sorry. I just can't stop thinking about you."

"Me, too."

He met her gaze. "Really?"

"Oh yeah."

Growling, he pulled her to him and kissed her again.

The smoldering kiss warmed her body from the top of her head to the tips of her toes and all the parts in between.

Gasping for breath, Sophie squirmed on the sofa, trying to snuggle closer to him. She wanted—no, *needed*—to caress him, to have her body pressed against his. Trembling hands raced up and down his back searching for purpose, for a way in to touch his skin. Moving down to the hem of his T-shirt, her hands streaked under the fabric and finally over the smooth marble of his back.

He moaned into her mouth as she traced a line up

and down his flesh with her short nails. Nibbling on her bottom lip, he moved down to her chin and up again to her mouth, sweeping his tongue between her lips to taste and tease her.

The man could kiss. With the hard press of his lips and the tantalizing way he moved his tongue over hers in a slow, torturous tango, he sent currents of white hot pleasure rippling over her body. And not once did she consider his fangs.

But that wasn't entirely true. She did think about them, especially when the slight brushing of them on her lips sent a wave of shivers down her back. She'd heard of the rapture a vampire's bite could bring. Would Kellen bite her if she asked? Did she have the courage to even ask such a thing?

With one hand wrapped in her hair and the other at the small of her back, he feasted on her mouth, tearing gasps of pleasure from her with every nip and nibble. She dug her fingers in while he moved over her chin and cheek with soft kisses that finally went to her ear.

"I can't get you out of my mind." He licked the side of her neck, brushing the tips of his fangs against her pulsing jugular. "You're a drug, and I'm addicted."

Letting her head fall back, Sophie dug her nails into his shoulders as he ravaged her neck, alternating between licking and sucking on her flesh. She'd surely have marks on her skin later, but at this moment she didn't care. Nothing mattered right now but the flush of heat racing over her body and the deep ache between her thighs.

Kellen moved down her body, yanking at the collar of her shirt to press his lips to her collarbone and lower. "Where's the bedroom?" He murmured, then trailed his tongue into the hollow of her throat.

"Down the hall…second…*ah!*…door on the right," she managed between gasps.

In one fluid motion, Kellen wrapped one hand around her waist and the other under her legs, then stood, swooping her up into his muscular arms. The man was strong and proved it by moving down the hallway without missing a beat or a single breath.

Still peppering kisses on her chin and mouth, he kicked open the door to her room, glided in and carried her to the bed. When he neared it, he knelt on the mattress and laid her down gently as if she were made of glass. But she didn't feel fragile or breakable. She felt fierce—emblazoned with a fiery passion so intense it nearly burned her from the inside out.

Kneeling beside her, he raked her body with his gaze. Even though she was still clothed, she felt the probing desire on her skin, as if he had touched her with the tips of his fingers. Biting her bottom lip, she reached for him, eager to pull him down to her body. She longed to feel his heavy weight on top of her.

But he dodged her hands, his eyes on hers, a roguish smile curling his sensuous mouth. "I want to see you. All of you." He licked his lips and a hot wave swept into her belly. "Lift your arms."

She did as he asked, raising her arms over her head.

Slowly, he lifted the hem of her shirt, over her stomach and up over her breasts, finally pulling the cotton past her arms. The cool air in the room sent shivers racing over her body. Instinctively, she went to cover herself with her hands, but Kellen held her arms back, desire lighting his eyes.

His gaze lowered to her cotton-covered breasts, and the light in his eyes sparked even brighter. He traced a finger over the top of her bra cups. She quivered under the slight caress. He was teasing her and doing a damn good job of it.

"It unhooks at the front," she breathed.

Chewing on his lower lip, in deep concentration, Kellen unhooked her bra with his thumb and forefinger. He brushed the halves aside and gazed at her adoringly. She could feel his hot breath on her nipples and she writhed in pleasure at the contradiction between the heat from his mouth and the cool of the room.

"You're more and more bewitching every time I see you." Leaning down, he took one rigid peak into his mouth.

Bowing her back, Sophie reveled in the pleasure surging through her as he sucked on her one nipple and rubbed the other with his fingers. After lavishing avid attention with his tongue and teeth to one aching peak, he moved onto the other, giving it equal consideration. When he was done and shifted his notice to her belly and navel, she was throbbing from every nerve ending.

He moved down her body to grip the band of her

cotton pants with his fingers. Pressing openmouthed kisses to her belly, Kellen pulled her pants down, her panties along with them. Sitting up, he tugged them down her thighs, over her knees and gently took them off her ankles, paying particular care with her injury.

With her pants tossed to the floor, he came back down to her, ravenous desire making his eyes glow. The way he regarded her set her blood aflame. Like liquid fire, it raced through her to end up between her thighs.

When he ran a tongue over his fangs and gazed down at the sprinkling of red hair at the juncture of her legs, she could hardly catch her breath. Closing his eyes, he pressed his nose to just above her pubic mound and inhaled her scent. She had to bite down on her lip to stop from mewling.

Head still bent, he nudged her legs apart and positioned himself between them. He placed a hand on each of her thighs, pressing his fingers into her flesh.

"Will you watch as I make you come?"

She nodded, her breath lodged in her throat. She was torn in sensual torture; wanting him to end her suffering, while at the same time desiring for him to prolong it.

Deliberately slow, Kellen made his way up her thighs. Rubbing his hands in circles, he inched closer to her sex, all the while watching her face.

Sophie's breath hitched in her throat as his fingers brushed over the light sprinkling of hair over her mound.

Like a gentle breeze, his hands swept over her, careful not to touch too much too soon. He was teasing her, and it was driving her insane.

The throb in her belly hovered close to the line between pleasure and pain. She itched to ease her own suffering. But she couldn't. He wouldn't let her. She was at his mercy. And she liked that.

As Kellen continued to tease her sex with light brushings of his fingertips, she ran her hands over her breasts, pinching and pulling on her nipples. Writhing on the bed, she arched her back and pushed her pelvis up in hopes that Kellen would ease her anguish. That he would lick and suckle her, and fill her with his fingers, his tongue, anything to urge her over the edge to a mind-blowing climax.

Her wishes did not go long unfulfilled. Lying down on his stomach between her spread legs, Kellen parted her with his thumbs. She could feel his hot breath on her intimate flesh as he nuzzled his face into her. Lightly at first, he trailed his tongue up and down her slick channel, swirling the tip as he reached her opening.

Heaving, Sophie thrashed about on the mattress. The torment of his tongue sent her soaring with flashes of pleasure. Each time he neared her throbbing nerve center she thought she'd suffocate from the torture of craving final release.

"Oh, Kellen, please," she moaned.

As if caving in to her wishes, he nudged her clit with

the tip of his tongue. She jerked up in response to the sizzling lash that whipped over her. With one hand, he pressed her down on the bed, keeping her still while he continued to lavish attention on her flesh. He lapped at her sex, suckling on it in between strokes of his tongue.

With ease, he slid two fingers into her, manipulating her with quick, hard thrusts. She could feel him pressing against her velvety flesh, as if in search for just the right spot. She prayed he'd find it and end her pleasurable agony.

The scorching heat between her legs was quickly nearing unbearable. Sophie was close to climaxing. The muscles in her belly and thighs tightened, preparing her for the overwhelming rush of ecstasy. A few more well-placed strokes and she'd tumble over the edge.

As he continued to thrust his fingers in and out, pushing as deep as he could go, Kellen suckled on her. She could feel his fangs scrape against her sensitive flesh as he sucked on her. She cried out from the sheer decadence and danger of it.

With one final stroke of his tongue, he pushed his fingers deeper, feeling her. All of her. Clamping her eyes shut against the sudden rush of bliss, she cried out as he found her spot, the fleshy mound on the inside of her channel. He pressed hard just as he clamped down on her nub with his lips.

She came in a searing liquid rush. White, blinding light flashed behind her eyes, and she couldn't catch her breath. Thrashing about, she grabbed onto Kellen's head, grasping for something—anything to release her from the electrifying hold he had her in. But he didn't succumb to her attempts. He continued to stroke his tongue over her and move his fingers inside, prolonging her orgasm.

Another commanding wave of pleasure crashed over her, stealing her breath again, drowning her. All the muscles in her body tightened, the nerve endings flared. She couldn't take any more. It was too much. She was certain to go mad, as sizzling hot flicks of rapture assaulted her body one right after another, until she couldn't think beyond the sensations controlling her.

Finally, she stopped fighting, and rode the waves of pleasure until she was spent.

Chapter 21

Kellen watched Sophie's face as she orgasmed. It was spectacular to see the way her eyes shifted from human to lycan and back again. It gave him an ego boost to know that he was able to give her so much pleasure that she had nearly lost herself to her beast.

Sleepily, she blinked up at him and smiled. Her whole face lit up as if a light bulb had switched on from the inside. She ran her hands over his head, and cupped his face, rubbing a thumb over his mouth.

"Take your damn clothes off and get on top of me."

Nipping on her thumb, Kellen didn't hesitate. He stripped off his T-shirt, tossed it over his shoulder and quickly shed his jeans. Leaning on his hands, he lifted himself over her, hovering so close he could feel her body heat enveloping him, and he kissed her.

Sighing, she parted her lips and swept her tongue over his. He loved the way she tasted—everywhere on her body. Like a fine wine, she enticed his tongue. Delectable and tantalizing. He'd remember her taste for the rest of his days.

As he nibbled on her lips, she dug her fingers into his back and pulled his body down. He couldn't resist the enticement any longer. He ached to lay with her, to be inside her. To have her heat wrapped so snuggly around him would be a pleasure he'd forever hunger for. Like he had told her before, she was addictive. And he was hooked.

The moment he covered her with his body, he could hear and feel her heart race. Like wildfire, it rushed through her veins, and he could sense every surge, anticipate them even. He itched to press his mouth to her neck and take a taste, just one tiny sip of her blood. But he knew one wouldn't be enough. He could imagine how delicious she would taste, like ambrosia, enticing, and addictive.

She ran her hands over his back, urgent and eager to possess. Cupping the back of his neck, she deepened the kiss, moaning into his mouth. He swallowed down each gasp, each heave of breath, willing and wanting to hear more of her groans, knowing he moved her to them. It was a powerful thing to pleasure a woman. Especially one as formidable as Sophie.

Throbbing for release, Kellen eased himself between her thighs and nuzzled against her sex. Obviously still sensitive, she jerked and writhed as he slid up and down her slick cleft. Finally, gloriously, she opened to him and he slid into her.

He closed his eyes against the savory assault on his body as he began to move inside her, finding a rhythm. She was so hot, so wet; it nearly did him in right there and then. There could never be another woman that felt so good writhing under him, responding to his every touch, every kiss.

He didn't deserve her.

His hands framing her face, Kellen kissed her hard. He wanted her to know how incredible she was, how humbled he was to be with her, thrusting inside her.

She wrapped her legs around him as he picked up the pace. With every thrust he dug his fingers into her shoulders. He had to hang on. He was free-falling without the safety of a parachute. He didn't know if he'd survive the fall.

Pressing kisses to her chin and down the side of her throat, Kellen thrust harder, faster, burying deep inside. She gasped as he rammed into her again and again, lifting her pelvis up to meet him each time.

His legs started to shake, the muscles clenched with strain. He was close, so close. Clamping his eyes shut, he drove into her as hard and as deep as he could. She raked her nails across his back and he knew there'd be divots in his flesh.

Then he heard the words that sent him spinning.

"Bite me," she whimpered. "Kellen, bite me."

Without hesitation, he did.

An explosion of taste and smell and color and sound erupted into his mouth and rushed through his body as her sweet blood touched his tongue. Intense sensations bombarded him all at once, sending him reeling.

In the same moment, he climaxed in a violent surge. Everything he ever was or ever would be poured out of him in that one, single, solitary moment. Kellen's mind tried to reach out for something to hold onto as he spun out of control. But there was nothing there to catch him as he whirled into oblivion.

For several minutes, Kellen thought he had died. Had actually truly and properly died. Not the undeadness some people believed vampires existed in. Blinking back the light blinding him, he saw he was truly alive for the first time in his life. He saw Sophie. And knew he had been reborn.

Smiling, she stroked her fingers over his sweaty hair and face, and then kissed his cheek. "I never thought it could be like that."

Unsure if he could move, he nuzzled into her neck and said, "Me, neither." His voice was hoarse and thick with desire. He'd only just had her, but he wanted her all over again.

Not wanting to crush her beneath his weight, Kellen rolled over onto his back and puffed out a breath. "I thought you damn near killed me, woman."

"Me? I'm not the one with the fangs."

He jerked up to an elbow and gazed down at her, concern making his heart clench. "Did I hurt you?" He fingered the wounds on her neck. They were already starting to disappear. A lycan's healing ability was no small thing, to be sure.

She shook her head and smiled, cupping his cheek. "Are you kidding me? It was…it was…amazing. I've never felt anything as incredible as that." She rubbed a thumb over his lips. "You can bite me any time you want."

He planted a quick kiss to her grinning mouth, then collapsed onto the bed on his back. She snuggled next to him and he wrapped his arm around her, glorying in the heat of her body. Content and fully satisfied, he realized he hadn't felt like that in…forever. Actually, he'd never felt like that.

If he never had to move from this spot on Sophie's bed, life would be perfect.

Head snug on his chest, Sophie trailed her fingers lazily up and down his sternum and sighed. He smiled to himself at her sigh of contentment. He almost felt like a damn hero. He chuckled at the thought.

"What's funny?" she asked, her fingers still making figure eights over his chest.

"I was thinking about how damn good I feel."

"Me, too. I haven't felt this relaxed in years."

"How's the ankle?"

"What ankle?"

Laughing, Kellen drew her closer and kissed the top of her head. "Do you think anyone would miss us if we stayed right here for the next week?"

"I don't know. I'm game if you are."

"We could pretend that I went home and you're taking a medical leave. No one would be the wiser."

She stiffened in his arm and he winced at the poor choice of words he used. The spell instantly broke around them. He could actually feel the magic dissipate in the cool air.

Her fingers paused on his skin and he could almost hear the wheels turning in her mind. "When this case is over you're going back to Necropolis, aren't you?"

"That was the plan."

She pushed up onto an elbow and looked him in the eye. "'Was,' or *is?*"

"I don't know."

"Would it make a difference to know that I'm falling in love with you?"

He kept her gaze. He didn't know what to say. Love was such a foreign thing to him. He didn't know if he'd ever really, truly experienced it in his lifetime.

He had strong feelings for Sophie, that was for sure, but he had nothing to compare it to. He had no basis of measurement. He didn't want to tell her something that might or might not have been true or real.

"Sophie, I—"

"Never mind." She rolled away from him, intent on getting off the bed, but he grabbed her arm before she could.

"No. Let me say something." He curved his palm around her face, forcing her to look him in the eyes. "You're important to me, Sophie. Don't ever doubt that. I don't have a lot of experience with love, but what I do know is that you matter more to me than anyone has before." He stroked her cheek. "Can that be enough for now?"

A tear rolled down her cheek and he caught it on the tip of his finger. He sucked the salty liquid off. "No tears. Not for me."

He pulled her to him and took her mouth with his. At first she hesitated to respond, but when he cupped the back of her neck and deepened the kiss, she sighed and wrapped her arm around him, taking him back down to the mattress.

Burying his hands in the yards of her silky red hair, he kissed her again and again. He didn't know if he could tell her that he loved her, but he knew he could show her, and he hoped that it would be enough for now.

Chapter 22

Sliding back the shower stall door, Sophie reached in and turned on the hot water. She was usually a morning person, but when she woke this morning, she still felt tired and groggy. Her muscles were sore, too. But she knew exactly what that was from. Lots of energetic sex.

When she had opened her eyes, she was surprised to see Kellen still asleep next to her. In her dreams, she had watched him get dressed and leave right after they had made love—just like last time. So, to feel him next to her, wrapped snugly in her blankets, a small smile tugging at the corners of his sexy mouth, had been strange and unexpected. But she couldn't deny that she had been pleased.

When the water was steamy hot, Sophie covered

her wounded ankle with a plastic baggie and then stepped under the vigorous spray, sighing as the healing heat beat upon her sore body. After soaking and soaping her hair, she turned, closed her eyes and let the water cleanse her face. She wished she had the luxury of pampering herself all day, but she and Kellen had to return to the lab—return to reality, and what it meant for them both, in their situation.

For all the strides the Otherworlders had made about their liberation and freedom to be who they were, to live their lives out in the open, she was forced to hide her feelings for a vampire. It made her angry and frustrated.

She shut off the water. Shaking her head, she slid the shower stall door open to grab the big cotton towel, but it wasn't where she hung it.

Kellen handed it to her. "Good morning." He wore a big grin and nothing else.

"Good morning." Suddenly feeling modest and shy, Sophie blushed. Trying hard not to ogle his beautiful naked body, she wrapped the big towel around her and stepped out of the stall.

He moved back to give her room, but hovered close as she stood in front of the big mirror. She went to grab the folded towel on the counter to dry her hair, but Kellen beat her to it. Nerves making her body quiver, she watched in surprise as he placed the towel on her head and started to rub her hair.

Smiling at her in the mirror as he dried her hair, he

leaned forward and placed a kiss on her shoulder, lingering a little to nibble on her skin. "Did you sleep well?"

She nodded, not trusting her voice. What he was doing with her hair felt almost more intimate than having sex. Grooming was a personal thing. Lycan mates in wolf form usually washed and groomed each other, but to have Kellen, a vampire, wanting to do this, made her body quake with more than just nerves.

When he was done drying, he tossed the towel over his shoulder and then ran his fingers through her long, wet strands. "Do you have a comb?"

"What are you doing?" she finally asked, her breath hitching in her throat.

"I want to comb your hair."

"Why?"

"Because you had a rough day yesterday, and I want to pamper you." His words were rushed and she could see he struggled with embarrassment. It made her smile just a little to know he was maneuvering in unknown waters, just as she was.

She handed him her comb.

With a knowing look, he took it and, holding on to the ends of her hair, set it at her scalp. He brought the comb down and through the strands, then up again to start over.

Sophie's knees wobbled a bit as the plastic teeth of the comb stroked her hair. The sensations zinging through her were glorious and unanticipated. Who knew that having a man combing her hair could be such a turn-on? Her thighs tingled in response.

Watching his face in the mirror, she suspected that he was experiencing similar responses. Eyebrow raised, his lips curled up into a mischievous grin. "This is surprisingly arousing."

She giggled as he pressed up against her back. There was no mistaking his desire. As the hard length of him dug into the swell of her buttocks, the tingle between her legs intensified into a full throb.

With every stroke of the comb through her hair, Kellen matched it with movements from his hips. He nuzzled closer to her until her pelvis hit the edge of the counter. Closing her eyes, she let her head fall back into his hands.

Soon his fingers replaced the comb and, starting at her scalp, he ran them through the strands. Once done, he placed his fingers on her head again, but this time, he moved them down, rubbing circles, massaging her scalp and then neck.

"Feel good?" She groaned in response and he laughed. "Feels good for me, too."

His hands continued down, caressing and massaging her neck. Fingers brushed against her jaw line, then lowered to her shoulders, where they paused.

"Open your eyes."

Slowly, she did as he asked.

With Kellen behind her, his hands resting on the curve of her shoulders, she stared at herself in the mirror. Eyes on hers, his hands moved down to the edge of her towel. He tugged at the cloth and, gripping a side in each hand, he pulled it apart to reveal her naked form beneath.

She shuddered as the terry cloth slid down her arms and landed in a heap at her feet.

With light, feathery touches, he trailed his fingers back up her body. Moaning, she leaned into him and raised one arm to hook around his neck, inviting him to take more.

Pressing his lips to the sensitive spot between her neck and shoulder, Kellen's hands became bolder. He trailed his fingers over her stomach and up toward her breasts, until finally, gloriously, he molded them with his palms.

Eyes glued to the mirror, she couldn't tear her gaze away from the image of her and Kellen together, his hands on her body, flicking and pulling on her taut nipples. She'd always been pleased with how she looked, but not once had she thought herself vain. But seeing herself, pale and naked, trembling against Kellen's body, reveling in her own pleasure, she thought herself stunning.

Jolts of fervent bliss rushed over her as Kellen nibbled on the side of her neck. His one hand moved down her body, circling her navel with just the tip of his finger, to then brush against her sex. She quivered at this briefest of a touch.

Gasping as he lowered his caresses, her knees nearly

gave out when he slid his fingers into the heat between her thighs.

"You're so damn beautiful. Do you know that?" he panted in her ear as he slid his fingers up and down her slick cleft. "Just looking at you makes me hard."

The muscles in her thighs and belly quivered as he stimulated her. A liquid ball of heat swelled deep inside, swirling like a tornado. It wouldn't take much more for her to climax.

Kellen moved his hand from her sex to grip her thigh. Pulling up, he bent her leg and set her heel on top of the counter. The motion and position spread her wide and she could clearly see the vivid color of her most intimate flesh.

The decadence of it washed through her like a fluid rush of liquid fire. Her heart hammered in her throat as Kellen's fingers slipped into her slick core, filling her.

He trailed his tongue over her ear and moaned. "Mmm, you're so hot. So wet."

Transfixed, she watched as he went from pumping his fingers inside of her, to rubbing her hard nub, and back again. Breath hitching in her throat, she could hardly stand. Hot, fevered pleasure rushed over her, through her. Every muscle in her body shuddered and quaked.

"I can't hold back," he groaned. "I need to be inside you now."

Shifting his position, Kellen cupped her with one hand, his other hand gripping her hip. Slowly, he entered her, filling her. She arched her back to take more of him in. She wanted—no, needed—him to fill her completely.

Once fully seated, he started to move, thrusting in hard and dragging out slowly as if to torture her with his delicious, languid pace. Although she desired him to hurry, to bury himself totally, Sophie bit down on her lip and let him have his way with her. Let him control the pace and dominate her pleasure.

Thrusting deep, he cupped her, sliding fingers along her core, rubbing at her nerve endings. She gripped his neck tight in anticipation. She was so near, hovering on the edge. She could taste the rapture in her mouth with each ragged breath.

His pace increased. Moaning, he rammed into her again and again, digging his fingers into her hips. She pushed back as he thrust forward. She couldn't control her body any longer, it wanted to take more, give more.

With one final grunt, Kellen drove in deep. Everything exploded around her. Sound and sight became a garbled kaleidoscope of sensation. She couldn't distinguish where she ended and he started.

Crying out, she spiraled down into a hot, swirling pool of pleasure. Under the intense bliss, she drowned completely, utterly, her breath knocked from her lungs.

After a few heavenly minutes, reason and rhyme finally returned to Sophie. She took in a shuddering breath and tried to move. Her leg still shook from the effort.

Chuckling, she slid it off the counter. "I feel like Jell-O."

"Mmm, I love Jell-O." Kellen pressed a kiss to her temple and nibbled her skin there.

She met his gaze in the mirror, wondering if he realized what he just said. By the spark in the dark depths, she imagined that he did, and it was no accidental exchange of words.

She smiled as he reached for her robe hanging on the back of the door and slid it over her, tying it securely at her waist.

"What a great way to wake up." He stretched his arms above his head.

Laughing, Sophie turned and swatted him with the wet towel.

A sudden knock at the front door shattered the magical spell between them. Sobering instantly, Sophie pulled the robe tighter and left the bathroom to see who was at the door.

There were very few people who knocked on her door. She prayed that none of those few were actually behind the ominous rap.

Chapter 23

While Sophie went to answer the pounding at her door, Kellen wandered back into the bedroom and slipped his jeans on. He decided to forego a shirt, and after a cursory glance in the bedroom mirror, he strolled down the hall and into the living room.

That had been his second mistake. The first was thinking he shouldn't put on a T-shirt.

Sophie stood in the living room, her shoulders hunched and on edge, next to another lycan. He didn't have to be introduced to know instantly it was her father, the alpha of her pack.

The man was shooting sparks from his eyes the second Kellen entered the room. The lycan had an overwhelming amount of power. Kellen sensed it in the air like an electrical current. This was one lycan he didn't think he ever wanted to mess with. Now he knew from where Sophie acquired her immense strength and endurance. Daddy dearest.

He pinned Kellen with an angry glare. "Is this him?"

"If you're asking if I'm the vampire Sophie is having a relationship with, then yeah, I'm him."

Sighing, Sophie ran a hand over her face. "Leon, this is Kellen Falcon. Kellen this is my father, Leon St. Clair."

Hand out, Kellen approached Leon. The lycan stared at him and didn't make a move to complete the gesture. "I suggest you shake my hand, Mr. St. Clair. You don't want to be rude."

That seemed to shake him a bit and he grabbed Kellen's hand, shaking it firmly. In that moment Kellen gauged Leon. It was obvious the man loved his daughter and wanted to protect her, most likely at all costs. If Kellen had a daughter, he wouldn't want her to date him, either. But if Sophie wanted him in her life he wasn't going to be bullied out of it.

She looked from one to the other. "This better not be a testosterone match. I'm not going to stand here and watch it, if it is."

"Sophie, I'm here because I'm concerned about you."

She crossed her arms. "No, you're here to tell me what I can and cannot do. Big difference."

"Sir, if I may—"

Leon wheeled on him. "What are your intentions toward my daughter?"

"Father…" Sophie started.

"I'm sorry? My 'intentions'?" Kellen stammered.

"Yes. Do you love her? Are you planning on marrying her? What about children? Lycans breed many children. It's our way to keep the pack functioning and healthy."

Kellen felt a hard lump forming in his throat.

"Can you even breed? I understand it's difficult for vampires."

"Look, what happens between Sophie and me is between Sophie and me and has nothing to do with you. I understand how pack politics work, but I'm not a lycan tied down by ludicrous rules about who I can have a relationship with."

"Exactly," Leon grunted. "You *aren't* a lycan, and that is exactly the problem here."

"Do you have a problem with vampires?"

"No. A couple of my closest friends are vampires."

"But we're not good enough to date your daughter, is that it?"

Leon went to open his mouth again, but closed it quickly, obviously careful of his next words.

"That's enough. Stop." Sophie's voice was commanding. It even made Kellen flinch a little. "I'm tired of hearing this. It's none your concern, Leon."

"It *is* my concern, Sophie. As your alpha and your father, it's my duty to ensure that you get everything you need to live a full and healthy life." He pointed at

Kellen. "What can you give her that will enable that to happen?"

Kellen opened his mouth then closed it just as fast. He had no clue what to say to the man, because he wasn't sure himself. He didn't know what he could offer Sophie that another man couldn't give her. He certainly couldn't give her a brood of children, if that's what she wished.

Thankfully, Sophie stood in between them, glaring at her father. "We're not having this conversation, Leon. You may leave. Kellen and I need to get back to the lab."

Leon went to open his mouth again, but the look on Sophie's face must have given him pause, because he quickly closed it, nodded, and walked out of the house.

When he was gone, Sophie turned to him. "Finish getting dressed. I'll make some coffee and we can go."

Too stunned by the conversation to say anything else, Kellen turned and went back to the bedroom to get dressed. He felt like a fool and a coward. He hadn't stood up for himself or for their relationship. He could just imagine what Sophie thought of him now. Too cowardly to stand up to her father, to defend their relationship—whatever it may be.

An hour later, with coffee cups in hand, Sophie drove them back to the lab. The only thing breaking the uncomfortable silence between them was the morning news on the radio talking about the bombings taking place around the city.

The moment they arrived at the lab, Gabriel intercepted them, and Kellen felt relieved by the interruption.

"Meeting in the conference room."

They followed the inspector to the room and both sat down at the table. Olena was already seated, drumming her long red nails on the table.

Gabriel took a seat at the end of the table. "The word came down that NORM has taken responsibility for the bombing at the lycan club."

Olena cursed. "There must be a faction inside the city."

"That's what it's starting to look like."

"What's going to happen?" Sophie asked. "Are they going to start shipping humans out of the city?"

Gabriel shook his head. "I don't think it's come to that—not yet anyway. There are a few leads that the superintendent is following. He'll let us know more when he knows more." He tapped the folder on the table in front of him. "Now, to our other bombings."

"Did they find anything at the Martin house?" Kellen asked.

Gabriel opened the file folder. "Nothing probative. Nothing to indicate that he's been building bombs."

"Has anyone been able to locate him?" Sophie asked.

The inspector shook his head. "He hasn't returned home, and the listing we had for his place of work turned out to be false."

"He's gone to ground." Kellen shifted in his chair. "He knows we're looking for him, and he's gone into hiding."

"We'll catch him," Gabriel said.

"Only if he wants you to." Kellen stood. "I want to go to his house, look around. Maybe there's something I can see that your guys didn't catch."

Gabriel shrugged. "If you think it will help."

"It might."

Sophie stood, too. "I'll go with you."

Frowning, Gabriel glanced from Kellen to Sophie. Kellen knew that look in the inspector's eyes. Disapproval and caution. He wanted to tell him he didn't need either.

"Get the keys out of evidence." Gabriel shut the file folder. "Call if you find anything." He tucked it under his arm and walked out of the room.

Olena patted them both on the back as she walked past. "Have fun, you two. Don't get caught with your pants down."

When everyone was gone, Sophie looked at Kellen. He smiled at her, trying to lighten the dismal mood that had come between them. "Ever feel like you're in high school all over again?"

She laughed. "Yes."

He gave her his arm. "Let's go make more mischief, shall we? See how many more tongues we can get wagging."

She wrapped her hand around his arm and smiled.

In an instant, relief settled over him like a snug, form-fitting sweater. He was falling in love with her, and anyone be damned if they didn't like it or weren't comfortable with it. He wanted to celebrate it. Love was so difficult to find that he didn't want to push it away because others couldn't accept it, including himself. For the first time in a long time, he felt like he had something to live for.

Chapter 24

The suspect's house turned out to be a quaint two-bedroom brownstone in a nice, quiet neighborhood. In Kellen's opinion, it was a perfect place for a bomber to hide. No one would ever suspect that one of their neighbors liked to build explosive devices and blow them up to kill people.

The house was virtually empty when they arrived. What little evidence there was had already been packaged and shipped to the lab for inspection, and the rest of the house was empty. It appeared that Louis Martin had lived meagerly while in this place.

There was no sofa or television or any other furnishings, except a simple chair and coffee table in the living room. The kitchen had no table. He imagined Louis probably ate at the bar counter, as a single wooden stool sat there alone.

"He didn't have much."

Kellen eyed the place intently. "I don't think he was planning on living long."

She glanced at him. "He had *Sangcerritus?*"

Kellen nodded. "I bet it was pronounced. Making him just a wee bit crazy in the old noodle." He tapped the side of his head with his knuckle.

Lowering her gaze, Sophie went back to searching through the kitchen. She reached for the cupboard, then paused as if remembering last time she went snooping in someone's kitchen cupboards. She swung around toward Kellen.

"Do you sense anything? Should I be worried about opening drawers?"

Pausing for a moment to listen to anything out of the ordinary, he eyed her once then shook his head. "Nothing to worry about in here."

"In here?"

"Yeah, I haven't searched the rest of the house yet." He gave her a twisted smile that he hoped eased her heart a little.

"Do you smell anything?" he asked, cruising around the empty dining-room area.

Lifting her nose in the air, she inhaled deeply, then looked at Kellen. He wondered what she smelled. What did he smell like?

Inhaling again, she seemed to sense something. She moved toward Kellen silently, and whispered in his ear, "Someone else is here."

"Are you sure?" he said in her ear.

She nodded, and gestured toward the hallway that led to the back bedrooms.

Taking her hand, Kellen moved toward the hall, back against the wall. Together, they slid along the wall, taking slow, measured steps so as to not announce their intent. When Kellen reached a doorway, he stopped and quickly peered in. He shook his head and they continued toward the two closed doors.

Before they reached them, Sophie yanked on his hand to stop him. Turning to her, he raised an eyebrow in question.

She whispered, "Let me go first. I have a weapon." She unholstered her gun and pushed off the safety latch.

"No, I don't think so."

"Don't be an idiot, okay? I know you're a tough guy. You don't have to prove it here."

He glanced at her gun, then at her face. He hated to admit it, but she was right. "Fine, but if something happens to you I'm going to kick your butt."

They switched positions so she could go in first, weapon poised and ready.

On the count of three, Sophie slowly turned the doorknob and pushed. Gun pointed, she peered into the room. It must have been empty, because she backed out, and then turned toward the next door.

Again she counted to three, but this time Kellen got anxious and he kicked open the door. It splintered into pieces as it crashed onto the floor. She rushed in, weapon up, but once more the room was empty.

Except for a small black box on the carpet.

She went to the open window and glanced out. "He must've just jumped out the window." Turning, she walked back toward the box on the floor.

"Don't touch it!" Kellen pushed her away from it.

She eyed him curiously as he circled the box and then crouched down next to it.

"Is it a bomb?"

He shook his head and picked up the small box, rubbing a hand over the top, remembering the feel of silk under his fingers. "It's a stone box. I have one just like it at home, except mine's blue."

"Did he leave it here on purpose?"

Standing, Kellen kept his attention on the box in his hands. "I know this guy. I have to. We were in the same ordnance company in Vietnam. We both have these stone boxes."

"Maybe he bought his recently. Maybe he ordered it online."

"No, not this box. I can see the detail that went into it." He opened the lid. "The inside is inlaid with bones. Water buffalo bones. This is authentic. The initials of the man who made it are carved in the corner. The same as mine." He spun around toward the bedroom window—and moved toward it, testing its lock and peering outside. "He was here. He left this for me. He wants me to know we have a connection."

She approached him and put a hand on his shoulder. "What's the connection?"

"I don't know. There are some bits and pieces of my tour in Vietnam that I don't remember. I always assumed it was because I didn't want to remember, like post-traumatic stress. But now I'm not so sure that's the reason."

"Did something happen to you there?"

He nodded. "I have *Sangcerritus,* so does Louis. We're connected, and it all relates to Dr. Bueller. He was there in Vietnam at the same time we were. He's a leading doctor on the disease. Maybe that's for a reason."

"You think you got the disease from the war? Like the conditions from Agent Orange?"

"Yeah, but I don't think mine was an accident from chemical warfare."

"Genetic experiments?"

Sweat dribbled down his forehead and neck. The temperature in the room seemed to be increasing exponentially. He rubbed at his head. His temples were starting to throb. "I found a book about genetics in Dr. Bueller's second residence. It was called *Super Soldiers.* There were some handwritten notes in it about vaccinations."

"*Mon Dieu,*" she gasped. "This is major."

"And motive. If Louis Martin realized what the doctor had done to him and others, maybe he took his own revenge."

Pain tore through his temple. Stumbling, he dropped the box and grabbed his head with both hands.

"Kellen!"

He could hear her voice, but it echoed in his head like ping-pong. Bouncing back and forth, making him dizzy.

Another jolt stabbed him and he went to a knee, unable to stay on his feet. Blinking back tears, his vision swam in and out. He was going to faint. He was floating in air. He couldn't keep his body from lifting. It was okay though, because he'd always wanted to fly.

Something cool touched his neck and forehead. The sensation brought him around, set his feet back on the ground. Panting, sweat dripping down his body, Kellen opened his eyes and focused.

Sophie crouched beside him, her hands on his head. She was speaking to him, but he couldn't hear her words. He tried to read her lips but found it too confusing. He just wanted to sleep. He was so tired.

He watched her face. She was so damn beautiful. Too stunning to even look at, most times. He could drown in the vivid pools of her eyes. He'd die a happy man.

Moving her hands over his head, she kept talking to him. He really wished he could hear her words. She had a sexy voice, one that made his gut clench and his knees weaken. He squeezed his eyes shut then opened them, his ears finally popping.

"You're going to be okay. I'm here, baby. I'll always be here."

Swallowing the lump in his throat, Kellen wiped at his mouth and the sweat soaking his face. He nodded. "I'm okay." He pushed to his feet. Wobbling a bit, he reached out for Sophie. She held on to his arm.

He hated being weak, especially in front of Sophie. "I'm fine now. You can let go. I won't fall."

Sophie rubbed her hand over his shoulder and down his arm to link her fingers with his. "I'm so sorry, Kellen. I can't imagine what it's been like for you to go through all of this."

He kept her gaze, wanting to wrap himself around her, to bury into her heat and find solace. She did that for him. Gave him a sense of peace. Being around her calmed him, soothed the maddening disease rushing to his head.

But would she be able to handle it when it got worse? When finally the disease took his mind completely and forced him to do and say things that he didn't mean. Was it fair for him to even expect her to?

Dropping his gaze, he looked at the box. "We need to find Louis before he hurts someone else."

"Do you think he will?"

He nodded. "I don't think he has any plans to stay alive for long. And he'll want to go out with a bang. Literally. I know I would."

Dropping his hand, Sophie took a distancing step back. She picked up the box from the floor and handed it to him. Did she sense him pulling away? If the dejected look in her eyes was any indication, she sensed everything about him. She knew he was putting up a wall. It was actually scary to have someone know him that well.

"We should get back to the lab and inform Gabriel about everything that's going on." She exited the bedroom and Kellen followed her out, all the way to the car, jumping into the passenger seat.

Sophie started the vehicle, then looked at him. There was an intense gleam in her eyes. "We'll get a citywide APB out on Louis Martin. If he goes to ground, we'll just dig him up."

Kellen smiled at that. She was fierce, his Sophie. He loved that about her, the fact that she could be hard when needed, one minute, and soft the next, made his heart clench.

His Sophie.

The significance of the thought wasn't lost on him. It was how he felt. He didn't know when it happened, but it had. He would always think of her that way, no matter what happened between them.

Chapter 25

The next three days were a comfortable haze for Kellen. After he informed Gabriel about all his suspicions and the information he gathered, the inspector put as much manpower as he could into locating Louis Martin. But with the city on the edge from the terrorist's attacks, he had other matters to attend to, as well.

So every day Kellen and Sophie put in hours at the lab, he with doing more research on Dr. Bueller aka Dr. Brenner, and genetics, and Sophie with a new caseload. Gabriel had become accustomed to him as had Olena, and as a group they had developed an odd symbiotic relationship.

At night, without voicing it, he and Sophie had

ended up back at Sophie's to eat and make love. Kellen only returned to his hotel room to get his bag and pay the bill, which he found out was already paid for by the Nouveau Monde crime lab.

The time they spent together was wonderful and not bogged down by talk of the case, or his disease or his eventual return to Necropolis. He suspected Sophie had made up her mind to enjoy their relationship for what it was. Even though he couldn't quite name it himself.

All he knew was that he was happy, truly content, without a desire for anything else. It was a strange sensation to have what he wanted—Sophie being at the top of his list. He tried not to think about tomorrow or next week, whether they caught Louis Martin, or not. He just wanted to enjoy every day as if it was his last.

By the incessant ticking in his head, that day was soon approaching.

Rubbing at his eyes, Kellen closed the computer application he was working in and leaned back in the chair. All his research wasn't getting him any closer to the truth about Dr. Bueller and what he had been up to in Vietnam. Maybe it didn't matter any longer. Even if he knew, what could that knowledge do for him? Maybe it was a fool's hope to discover the truth. But hope was there, regardless. Sophie did that for him.

The overhead speaker crackled to life. "Kellen Falcon to the reception area. You have a visitor."

Surprised, Kellen stood and wandered out of the

room. A visitor? He didn't know anyone in Nouveau Monde, except those in the crime scene team.

As he walked down the hall, Sophie popped out of one of the rooms, smiling.

"Hey." He returned her smile.

"I heard you have a visitor."

He shrugged. "Beats me who it could be. Maybe Caine flew over, thinking I needed some help or something. He's an utter control freak."

They walked side by side down the hall to the reception area. Kellen opened the door for Sophie and followed her through. He approached the main desk and smiled at the receptionist.

She nodded toward a short, dark-haired man standing in the middle of the foyer, his back turned toward them.

Alarm bells went off in Kellen's head. Something was wrong. He could feel it crawling over his skin. He turned toward Sophie to warn her, of what he wasn't sure, but it was too late.

The man turned around to face them. In an instant Kellen knew who it was.

"Louis."

Sophie tensed beside him and grabbed his arm.

The man nodded. "Hallo, Kellen." His accent was a thick brogue. Scottish most likely. He must have spent all these years after the war in Europe to develop the accent.

He unzipped his thin nylon jacket. Underneath, a

dozen red and blue wires stuck out. It was what Kellen feared. Louis was wired with explosives—by the looks of it, enough to blow up half of the building.

Sophie gasped. Kellen pushed on her arm. "Get out of here."

"She stays." Louis opened his right hand to reveal a detonation switch.

Kellen did a quick survey of the reception area. So far it was fairly empty. Charlotte, the receptionist, was at her desk, he and Sophie and two officers that had joined them, their suspicions getting the better of them. They both had their weapons out and pointed at Louis.

Louis swiveled toward one officer. "Lock the main doors. Don't let anyone else in here."

The officer hesitated for a moment. It looked like he was deciding whether or not to shoot Louis in the head.

Louis must have assumed the same thing, because he said, "I wouldn't recommend it, boy-o. It doesn't matter where you shoot me, I'll push the button. Because I'm a vampire, even a head shot will give me roughly two seconds to press my thumb down. Then everything will go boom. Including you, your mate and half this building."

After glancing at the other officer, he ran to the doors and flipped the lock. The other officer moved toward the door separating the lobby from the main lab and turned the lock, then went to the other door that led to the main police headquarters and bolted that, as well.

That left the six of them in the lobby.

"Why don't we let the two ladies go, Louis?" Kellen purposely used the word "we," hoping Louis would make a personal connection with him. But he felt their connection went beyond personal—they were tied together from something that happened almost forty years ago.

Louis glanced at Charlotte, then at Sophie. "Yeah, why not? It's not going to make a difference either way."

Sophie squeezed Kellen's arm and murmured, "I'm not leaving without you."

Smiling, he pressed a kiss to her forehead. "It's okay. I'll be fine. He doesn't want to kill me. Do you, Louis?"

Louis shrugged as if he didn't have a care in the world.

"Charlotte," Kellen called. The receptionist looked at him, her eyes wide with fear. "Come on out. Go with Sophie."

Trembling, Charlotte stumbled out from behind the large counter and walked toward them. She grabbed onto Sophie, tears starting to roll down her cheeks.

Sophie patted her hand. "It'll be fine." With one last fleeting look at Kellen, she guided Charlotte to the lab doors, flipped the lock and went through. Kellen locked the door behind them.

Before Sophie led Charlotte down the hall away from the potential danger, she turned and mouthed three words to him, "I love you."

Pressing his lips together, he just nodded, unable to reciprocate in the way he wanted. He'd give anything right about now to hold Sophie in his arms and feel the press of her body heat and hear the rush of her heartbeat.

"That's nice," Louis commented from behind Kellen. "To have someone who loves you."

Turning, Kellen walked towards Louis. "Yeah, it's great. You don't have anyone right now worrying about you?"

"Nah, not with this craziness swirling in my noggin'." He knocked himself in the forehead with the knuckles on his left hand. "I'm not particularly pleasant to be around right now."

"It's bad?"

"You have no idea." He cocked his head. "No, I guess you would know. The doc sure messed with us something awful, didn't he?"

"I don't know, Louis. I'm playing catch-up here."

Louis glanced around the lobby. Noticing the sofa and chair in the corner away from the plateglass window, nodded toward it. "Do you mind if we sit down? I'm beat. I haven't been getting much sleep lately."

"Sure." Together, they moved toward the sofa. Louis sat on the edge facing the lobby area. Kellen sat on the chair. "How about we let the two officers get out of here so we can talk?"

"Nah, I need some reassurance that they aren't going to rush in here and take me out. For some reason, I don't think they'd make those concessions for just you and me, two diseased vampires who are going to die anyway." He motioned toward the other half of the sofa. "Why don't you two chaps join us? This sofa is very cozy."

After hesitant glances at each other, the two officers made their way over and sat down. Kellen noticed they were both sweating, their eyes nervously shifting back and forth between him and Louis. By the looks of them both, he didn't think they'd been on the force long. They both had an air of inexperience and fear.

Kellen nodded to them. "Just relax, fellas. Louis just came to talk."

"Yeah, I just came to talk to my old mate Kellen here. We have a lot to discuss. Old times to go over." He shifted in his seat, trying to reach in his right coat pocket with his left hand. He looked at Kellen. "Do me a favor, mate, reach in and get my pack of ciggies."

As Kellen leaned forward, he eyed the rig around Louis's torso. It looked like four pounds of C-4 explosives fastened to Velcro straps and wrapped in three thick strips around his chest and stomach. Glancing at the wires, he tried to figure out what was attached to what, but he didn't have enough time to gauge it. He wasn't quick enough to pull them all before Louis pressed the detonator.

Louis grinned as Kellen slid his hand into the man's pocket. "Sorry, Kellen, I made sure there was no way you could disarm me. I know how fast you are. But it won't be enough."

Kellen grasped the pack of cigarettes and took them out, along with a Zippo lighter. He shook one out for Louis. "Hey, you can't blame me for looking. I really don't want to die today."

Louis took the offered smoke and put it in his mouth. Kellen lit the cigarette and sat back.

He blew out a couple of smoke rings. "Yeah, but you're going to soon enough. The good doctor made sure of that."

"I heard he was working on a cure."

"He was. He and a Chinese doctor named Shen Li were close to the answers when Brenner pulled the plug on their research, taking what he could and leaving Li with nothing." Leaning his head back on the sofa, he blew some more smoke rings, then continued, "Brenner realized there was too much money to be made by treating *Sangcerritus* than in curing it."

"Is that why you killed him?"

Louis nodded and took another drag on his cigarette. "I went to him before and begged him to continue with the research. I told him I knew about the experiments he did on us in the war. How he was trying to make super soldiers, but instead gave us this disease. He just patted me on the head and told me to be a good boy and keep my mouth shut."

"What about this other doctor? Was he involved in the initial tests in Vietnam?"

Louis shook his head. "Nah, Dr. Li's too young to have been in Vietnam."

Kellen could just imagine how furious Louis must have been to know that Brenner purposely injected something into them without their knowledge, and inadvertently gave them a lethal disease—and then tried to profit from it in the end. Kellen was shaking with fury now, as he heard all that he suspected being spelled out for him.

"Why didn't you expose him?"

He shrugged. "I was going to, but killing him seemed like a much better plan."

"You killed three other people."

"I know. That was a bugger." He flicked his cigarette butt on the floor and ground it out under his boot heel. Shifting again, he reached into his left jacket pocket and came away with something. He tossed it to Kellen.

It was a small key.

"That's to a safety deposit box downtown in the main Nouveau Monde Bank of Europe. You'll find all your answers there, mate."

Kellen glanced down at the key, then back at Louis. Something had changed in the vampire. A kind of peace had settled over him. He didn't like what it could mean. "What about you? We can find this cure together. It doesn't have to end badly."

He smiled again. "You're an optimist, Kellen. That's a rare find in a vampire."

"I know the superintendent. I can talk to him about reducing your sentence. You're a vampire. A life sentence is what, forty years? You can still have a long life ahead of you, Louis."

Louis glanced at the two officers. "Look at him, lads, trying desperately to save my life. You're a good chap, Kellen." His gaze returned to Kellen. "Tell you what—I'll let you be a hero for your lady. You can save some lives." Reaching with his left hand, he pulled two wires out of the detonator strapped to his hand. He unwrapped the trigger and tossed it to Kellen.

Unbelieving, Kellen looked down at the detonator in his hand. Squeezing it tight, he glanced up at Louis. Something was wrong. The man would never have walked in here dressed literally to kill, then give up. It didn't make any sense.

He met Louis's gaze and it became clear. Except it was too late to do anything about it.

Faster than he could blink, Louis reached across the sofa, unsnapped and unholstered the officer's gun and pressed the muzzle under his chin, angled at his head. He smiled again at Kellen. "You can save lives. All of them but mine."

Yelling, Kellen leaped toward the sofa, intent on grabbing the gun. But he wasn't fast enough.

The blast of the gunshot echoed in his head.

It was a sound he would never forget.

Chapter 26

When Sophie heard the sound of a gunshot, she thought her heart had actually imploded. A pain so sharp, so intense, ripped through her that she found her legs wobbling like jelly when she ran down the hall to the door separating the lab and the lobby.

The lock didn't keep her from the room.

She grabbed the handle tight and twisted, snapping the entire locking mechanism and yanking it off the door. She was racing across the lobby floor before anyone else had reacted. The bomb squad tried to evacuate her earlier with the rest of the team, but she had refused to go. After one of them received a solid punch to the jaw, no one else bothered to reason with her.

When she spotted Kellen across the room, blood splattered over his face and T-shirt, she nearly went down to her knees. But after another perusal of the scene, she noticed Louis Martin slumped on the sofa. Obviously the blood didn't belong to Kellen.

As she threw herself into his arms, relief surged through her like a tsunami. Tears trickled down her cheeks. He hugged her tight and pressed his lips to her temple, drinking her in.

"Please don't do that to me again," she breathed, digging her fingers into his back, too scared to let go of him.

He smoothed a hand over her hair and murmured into her ear, "I promise I won't meet up with another man with explosives taped to his body and a death wish." He pressed his lips to the sensitive spot just below her earlobe.

She sighed and hugged him tighter. When she had escorted Charlotte out of the lobby, Sophie didn't know if she'd see Kellen alive again. Standing in the background, not knowing what was going on, was the hardest time she'd ever experienced in her life.

The thoughts that had raced through her mind had been staggering, nearly immobilizing. All she could picture was another bomb going off and Kellen being ripped to pieces by the debris—and her left with only pieces to put back together.

"Oh God, Kellen, I thought I lost you."

Leaning back, he cupped her face with his hands

and looked deeply in her eyes. "I'm not going anywhere, Sophie. For as long as you want me, I'm here."

"I want you for a long time."

"Then no matter what, I'll always come back to you,
my Sophie." He kissed the tip of her nose.

She smiled and, cupping the back of his neck, pulled
him down to her mouth. She kissed him long and hard
until her toes curled and her thighs tingled. It was a
good kiss. A kiss full of possibilities.

The rest of the team arrived and they worked the
crime scene. Statements were taken from Kellen and
the two stunned officers. The coroner had come and
gone, the obvious manner of death listed as a suicide.

It had seemed surreal to Sophie to have it end this
way, with Louis's death. But the case was closed. They
had their bomber. Unfortunately, it didn't feel like the
resolution had been a win. Louis had been a victim, too.
How would he be vindicated?

An hour later, Sophie and Kellen stood in the lobby
of the Nouveau Monde Bank of Europe talking to the
manager about a safety deposit box. He led them to the
private room, left, and then came back with the steel
box. He set it on the table in front of them and left
again.

Kellen opened it with the key. Inside were several
file folders full of information. He took them out and
flipped through the pages. Sophie saw pictures, charts,
reports and handwritten notes.

"Where did he get all this?"

"I think most of this is the doctor's research notes. This is what he got from the doctor's second apartment. That's where he was doing all his research."

She wrapped her arm around his waist and hugged him. "This is great. All of this can help you find a cure."

He nodded, but his attention was on the research papers. "I guess there's a doctor in China who was working on the cure with Dr. Brenner." He pointed to some information written on a page. "Here it is, Dr. Shen Li. I can take all of this to him. He can continue with it."

"That's fantastic, Kellen. I'm so happy for you."

Setting the folder down, he gathered her in his arms and hugged her tight, lifting her off the floor. "I finally feel like there's some hope. I can finally get on with my life."

She hugged him back and, smiling, gave him a smacking kiss on the mouth. But she didn't feel the joy behind it. A feeling of uncertainty fluttered in her stomach. She was overjoyed for Kellen, but somehow she thought that his search for a cure would ultimately lead him away from her. It was a selfish thought, but she couldn't stop it from setting up camp in her head.

She had just found him, the man she'd been searching for, and she wasn't ready to give him up.

When they returned to the lab, Sophie allowed Kellen his space and privacy to go through the files. For the next three hours, he poured over the information in the file folders from the safety deposit box. All the experiments conducted in Vietnam were noted in detail by living subject. His file just happened to be the thickest and the most up-to-date.

Brenner had been keeping tabs on Kellen since his honorable discharge from the army. There were pictures of Kellen over the years, a copy of his application to the OCU and medical records from his doctor in Necropolis. It appeared that he was the last test subject to be diagnosed with *Sangcerritus*. His immune system seemed to be the strongest. But it eventually would fail, as did all the others.

All the test subjects—over one hundred of them— had been administered the experimental serum through the hepatitis vaccination by an unassuming administrator, a pretty nurse, in his case. Because vampires were already stronger, faster and didn't get killed easily, the serum was supposed to increase all of that, plus mental alertness and healing capabilities. With those heightened traits, a soldier could go on longer without sleep, be stronger and faster in the field and not wound so easily…a super soldier.

The doctor naturally didn't account for long-range side effects, or just didn't care. Vampires, after all, have stronger constitutions, and soldiers can be replaced.

Kellen hoped that Dr. Shen Li didn't share that attitude. The Chinese doctor was Kellen's last and only hope to be cured. He had done some checking on the Internet and located the doctor in Shanghai. But he had yet to call him. For some reason, Kellen was afraid to phone.

What if Dr. Shen Li didn't want to, or couldn't, help Kellen? What if he didn't make it to Shanghai in time?

That was the one idea that frightened him the most. Time. What if it had already run out?

Rubbing a hand over his face, he closed the file in front of him and leaned back in the chair to stretch. The past twelve hours had been harrowing to say the least. Watching Louis die had been tragic and unnecessary. Louis could have been saved, but he had lost all hope for his future. A hope for something better.

And maybe if Sophie hadn't come into his life when she did, Kellen would have felt the same way.

He had been traveling on a road of self-destruction. It was just a matter of where he would have met his end. But now he didn't have any desire to stop searching and give up. Sophie had given him meaning and a purpose.

Just thinking about her made his gut clench.

Glancing at the wall clock, he decided it was high time for a break, and if he had his way, it would be with a pleasant distraction, like a pretty lycan with icy blue eyes. He picked up the phone on the desk, intent on calling Sophie's cell phone, when Olena strode into the room in a whirlwind of energy.

"Get on your dancing shoes, Kellen, we're going out tonight."

"Excuse me?"

"I already talked to Sophie about it. She's up for a little fun."

"Really?"

She put her hand on her hip. He was starting to realize it was a typical Olena tactic. "Don't be a party pooper. Besides, it's my birthday. It's not every day a girl celebrates her two hundred and seventy-seven…ish birthday."

He chuckled. "You're right. That is a milestone."

"Anyway, you can have fun thoroughly intimidating my date."

"Who's the lucky guy?"

"François."

Kellen nearly sputtered. "You're going out with Frank? Is he even legal?"

She pouted. "Of course. He's a respectable twenty-one. What can I say? I like my men young."

Shaking his head, Kellen stood. "Okay, cougar, let's go have some fun."

Olena's idea of fun truly did involve dancing shoes.

She'd booked the four of them a table at a popular salsa club downtown called Casa de Musica, the Music House. It was packed and noisy, and Kellen loved it. Especially with Sophie at his side.

As they all stuffed themselves with great, Cuban-influenced cuisine, they talked and laughed like old friends. Frank was surprisingly witty and full of charm. Kellen's fondness for him grew throughout the evening, especially with the way he catered to Olena. The boy witch was definitely smitten with the vampiress.

And the boy had moves out on the dance floor.

Grabbing his hand, Sophie snuggled next to him as they watched Frank and Olena spin and shimmy around the room. "Who knew that François could dance?"

"I would never have guessed," Kellen chuckled, then turned to her. "Care to give them a run for their money?"

Her eyes widened. "I thought you didn't dance?"

"I don't usually, but that doesn't mean I *can't* dance." Standing, he pulled her to her feet and spun her around once. "I can be pretty light on my feet when I want to be."

He guided her onto the dance floor, pressing a hand to the small of her back and holding her other hand up and to the side. The short *wha-wha* of a saxophone and the one-two thump of bass started the next song—a mambo.

Quick-quick-slow, Kellen moved Sophie around the floor to the sensual beat. He pressed her close to his body as he moved his hips with the swift motion enunciated in the traditional mambo dance.

He could feel the change in her breathing patterns as they danced. Her heart rate went up as he moved his hand up and down her back. Dancing was an aphrodisiac, and they were both feeling the effects. He wondered how soon they could part company with Olena and Frank and make their way back to Sophie's for more body language.

"You definitely have the moves, Kellen Falcon."

He grinned, reveling in the way her body brushed against his. He was growing hard just by having her so near. She made him feel like a damn teenager, with an out-of-control libido. A feeling he could get used to—easily.

"I spent some time in Cuba." He spun her once, then back. "Wasn't much to do but drink and dance."

She laughed as he, pressing close, spun them around in a circle. "There's so much about you I don't know."

Brushing his lips against her temple, he murmured, "You know what matters."

She sighed as he ran his hand down the swell of her buttocks to the back of her thigh, and slowly raised her leg to his waist. Cupping her back with his hands, he bent her at the waist, dipping her low, his mouth a breath away from her breasts. The movement was torturously slow, and he found his own heart racing.

He brought her up quickly, so they were face-to-face. Her eyes were wide, her lips parted. Keeping her gaze, Kellen brushed his lips against hers. He'd never grow tired of seeing the spark in her eyes. She was breathtaking; and he was lost to her. He needed to tell her before he misplaced his nerve.

"Sophie," he breathed. "I—"

She pressed her fingers against his lips and smiled. "It will keep, Kellen. If you feel so strongly tomorrow, tell me then. Tonight, I just want to dance."

Cupping her face, Kellen took her mouth in a hard,

passionate embrace. The kiss made his knees weak and his gut churn, as if a thousand butterflies had set up camp. He could feast on her forever, glorying in the taste of her. The thought of forever didn't scare him any longer. He had to tell her, it couldn't wait until tomorrow.

A tap on his shoulder gave him pause.

Hands still wrapped around Sophie, Kellen turned in surprise. Duncan Quinn stood, hands fisted at his sides, glaring at them both.

"You and me have a little business to settle."

He could feel Sophie tense in his embrace. To effectively block her from Duncan, Kellen moved forward, linking a hand with hers.

"This is not the time or place, Duncan," Sophie said.

"I'm not talking to you, woman. I'm talking to your filthy vamp boyfriend."

A few dancers on the floor stopped to watch what was going on. Including Olena and François.

"Why are you not dancing?" Olena asked, her voice friendly, but Kellen sensed a change in her demeanor. She was as on edge as he was.

"Mr. Quinn here seems to have a problem."

Sophie moved past Kellen before he could stop her, and got in Duncan's face. "I suggest you leave now, Duncan, or I'll inform Leon about your behavior."

He smiled at her, but it wasn't friendly. It was a predator's grin. "Leon's on my side with this. He doesn't want that bloodsucker anywhere near you."

Moving so quick he was blurred, Kellen had Sophie

tucked behind him and he stood toe-to-toe with Duncan, releasing some of his power. Duncan shrunk back a little at Kellen's burst of energy.

"You know I can kill you in a blink of an eye, don't you?"

Duncan licked his lips but stood his ground. "You don't scare me. I've taken down bigger and meaner vampires than you."

"I don't want to fight you, Duncan. What happened before was unfortunate, but it's over."

"It's not over until you're gone."

"That won't change the fact the Sophie doesn't want you. You won't get her by default. It'll be her choice."

"I don't care anymore." He smirked. "She's used goods now, anyway."

Fury swirled through Kellen like a typhoon. Tightening his fists, he leaned forward, preparing to smash Duncan in the face. But something in his periphery caught his eye.

Everything, including people, tables and chairs started to waver behind Duncan. As if caught in heat waves, they rippled back and forth.

His stomach dropped and his heart lurched into his throat. It couldn't be happening. Not here. Not now. Oh God! Please no!

As if in slow motion, Kellen swiveled toward Sophie. She looked up at him, her eyes suddenly getting wider by the second. By his actions, she knew.

He grabbed her hands. "Get out! Grab Olena and Frank and get out!"

Like a coward, Duncan took that moment to attack.

His first punch landed squarely across Kellen's jaw. He felt the blow all the way to his feet. But it wasn't enough to take him down. Kellen was too pumped up on adrenaline to fall.

Kellen successfully blocked Duncan's next punch, then, pinning both arms to his body, he sandwiched the lycan in a bear hug. Duncan struggled but Kellen kept him there. "There's a bomb, Duncan. You need to get out. Now."

"What? You're insane, vampire. Your disease has finally taken you over the edge."

"Listen to me, asshole," Kellen bit out. "This place is going to explode. We need to get these people out of here."

Duncan looked around, panic slowly starting to take root. "I don't believe you."

"I don't care what you believe." He let Duncan go, pushing him back. The lycan stumbled, then landed on his butt on the floor.

Kellen swiveled around and started to shout, trying to be heard over the thumping music. "Everyone get out! There's a bomb!"

Thankfully, he saw Sophie herding Olena and Frank to the door. Mentally, he shouted to her to hurry, there wasn't much time. He could already feel the blast waves rippling through the room. The explosion was going to be devastating. A lot of people were going to die. He prayed to God that Sophie wasn't one of them.

Some people paused in their movements and glanced at him. He yelled again as he moved toward Sophie, keeping her in his sight, too scared to lose her in the crowd.

"Get out of the building! There's a bomb!"

This time some people heard him loud and clear. Panic flashed across their faces. They started toward the exit, some ran, others walking fast.

It wasn't long before alarm swept the room, and, like a herd of cattle, the patrons rushed the exit, pushing and shoving in their manic urge to get out. He didn't blame them—he wanted out just as much. He didn't want to die after all that he'd been through, and after finding Sophie. It would be a cruel irony.

Kellen moved with the crowd, keeping his eyes on Sophie. She was just about at the door. He sent a silent prayer for her to hurry. He couldn't survive if something happened to her. He wouldn't want to.

The air pressure around him started to drop. His head throbbed, his heart pounded. He could barely breathe. It was happening.

The timer had reached zero.

Looking up, he watched Sophie as her hand pushed at the exit door. It opened and she started through, but before she was gone she turned and met his gaze. And in her eyes he saw everything he needed to. She loved him—and would for an eternity.

"Sophie," he whispered.

She disappeared out the door.

Shouts behind him turned his head. He saw Duncan standing near the dance floor, looking around in confusion, others brushing past him to get out of the building. He was making no effort to get to an exit. Their gazes met, and Kellen pushed back through the crowd toward him.

"Come on, Duncan!"

In a flash of white, blinding light, and with a pulse-pounding metallic roar, everything around him exploded.

Chapter 27

Everything was black. Sophie struggled to wipe at her eyes. Was there something covering them? She wiped until finally, blessedly, pinpoints of light pierced the darkness. She blinked rapidly, trying to clear her vision.

Someone was talking to her, but Sophie couldn't make out their words. It was all garbled, as if spoken underwater. Turning her head, she tried to find the person speaking to her, but everything was blurry.

Hands held her head. A spot of white light swung back and forth before her eyes. She lashed out at it, but other hands grabbed her arms, pinning her so she couldn't move.

"Sophie? Sophie? It's Gabe. You're going to be okay."

His voice came to her as an echo. Was she in a cave? Why couldn't she see him?

"Take her to the hospital. I'll search for the others."

What others? Sophie struggled against her restraint. Then it hit her like a sledgehammer in the stomach.

The club. The bomb. Olena and François.

Kellen. Oh, her wonderful vampire, Kellen.

"Kellen!" she shrieked and fought against the leather straps keeping her down on the stretcher.

Gabriel's face came into view. He cupped her face, his eyes were glassy. Had he been crying? "You need to relax, Sophie. They'll take you to the hospital. You're injured. You need to heal."

"No," she moaned, tears rolling down her cheeks.

"Olena and François are alive. They have been taken to the hospital, as well."

"Kellen. I want to know where he is."

Gabriel stared her in the eyes for a moment, then pressed a kiss to her forehead. The action told her everything she needed to know.

"Take her to the hospital."

As the medics wheeled her toward the ambulance, she kept her gaze on Gabriel. He watched her until they lifted her into the vehicle. His head down, he walked away and into the destruction that had once been the Casa de Musica.

She screamed and sobbed and kicked in fury. The medics tried to calm her, but she wasn't listening. A rage ripped through her without mercy, tearing and stabbing at her. She called to Death to take her, to end her pain. But the bastard didn't. She struggled futilely until she felt a prick on her arm, and the darkness took her once more.

Smacking her lips and groaning at the horrid taste in her mouth, Sophie opened her eyes to the white ceiling and muted lights above.

She was in a hospital. She'd recognize the smell of disinfectant, medicine and sweat-dampened cotton sheets anywhere.

Craning her neck, she looked around the room. A yellow flannel curtain surrounded her bed, so she didn't see much but the IV stuck in her hand. The constant drip of the fluids from the bag made her head ache. It echoed in her ears like loud, crashing cymbals.

Without moving too much, she tried to gauge her injuries. Looking down the length of her body, which was covered by a white flannel blanket, she noticed the lump under the sheet near her ankle. She obviously had a new cast on it. She likely re-broke the healing bone trying to scramble out of the building with about fifty people pushing on her back.

Shifting a little to get comfortable, pain ripped over her torso. She guessed one or more ribs were broken. She likely had a ton of bruising and maybe a few lacerations.

She closed her eyes against the memory of broken

glass and wood, and flying pieces of cement and other materials raining down on her. The sound of the explosion rattled in her head again. Biting down on her lip, she tried to stem the tears from gushing. She'd been lucky to get out alive.

Others hadn't been.

An image of Kellen flashed in her mind and her heart compressed so tightly she struggled to breathe. Groaning, she took in air. But she felt like dying. The pain of his loss seared through her deeply, burning her to the bone. God, it hurt so badly, she dug her nails into the palms of her hands to combat the agony.

But she knew nothing could possibly lessen it.

The curtain around her bed rustled then parted. Gabriel came through.

"Hey." He patted her leg as he sat on the edge of her bed. "Do you need some water?" He reached for the plastic cup on the swiveling table attached to her bed.

She shook her head and turned so he wouldn't see her tears, her pain so clearly etched onto her face. "How long have I been out?"

"Twelve hours. The doctor says you're going to be fine. You're such a quick healer he suspects you'll be on your feet in a day or two."

She remained silent. She didn't care one way or another whether she healed or not. It all didn't matter. Without Kellen nothing mattered.

"Olena is already out. She's a tough cookie. François, on the other hand, is still in intensive care." He sighed. "A witch's physiology is much like a human's. Harder to heal."

"Please leave, Gabe. I don't feel like company right now."

He grabbed her leg and squeezed, getting her attention. She turned toward him, intent on telling him to go to hell.

"Kellen's alive, Sophie."

She frowned at him and shook her head, unable to form any coherent words. He couldn't possibly be telling her the truth. Was this his idea of a cruel joke?

Sliding off her bed, he grabbed the curtain and pulled it back. There was another bed beside hers. Kellen lay there under the blankets—still, eyes closed and hooked up to three machines.

Her heart leapt into her throat. Struggling with the tube sticking out of her, she rolled over in her bed, intent on getting up and going to him. But her limbs weren't agreeing with her goal. They were leaden and stiff from severe bruising.

Gabriel pushed her back into the bed. "He's alive but unconscious."

She stared at the oxygen mask fitted over his nose and mouth. "He's not breathing?"

Gabriel shook his head. "I think that possibly he's in a self-induced coma, meant to heal. I've heard of vampires doing that when their injuries are too severe."

"What kind of injuries?"

He paused and she knew he was gauging how much information to share with her. "He has a punctured lung and a lot of internal damage. The doctors are uncertain of exactly what they can do for him."

She rolled onto her back, and sighing, shut her eyes against the constant well of tears. *Kellen was alive.* She had to grasp onto that, even if his unconscious state gave her no relief. He was alive and she wouldn't let him die, no matter what.

She opened her eyes and looked at Gabriel. He was watching her intensely. Sorrow swam in his eyes. "What else? I know you're keeping something else back." Her voice sounded flat in her ears.

"Duncan's dead."

Pressing her lips together, she tried to keep the grief inside. More tears rolled down her temples to drip onto the pillow. She never loved Duncan, but the pain of his death stabbed her inside. He had been a friend once, and a member of her pack. No matter his last actions and words, he deserved her grief. No one should have to die like that.

Gabriel patted her leg, but she felt as though he did it as much for himself as for her. He had known Duncan, had been friendly with him and even spent some nights running together in the park. They hadn't been close like brothers, as Gabriel hadn't been one of the pack, but there had been some camaraderie, enough that the pain of his death had to cut him inside, too.

"It looks like Kellen tried to get to him, but he was too far back in the crowd to save. A ceiling beam fell on him and broke his back."

Words failed her. She nodded, letting him know she understood his pain and thanked him for telling her.

"Your father's chomping at the bit to see you." She opened her mouth to protest, but Gabriel patted her leg and continued, "I'll tell him he can't stay long."

"Thank you, Gabe."

Standing, he moved forward and leaned down to kiss her forehead. "You're welcome. Heal yourself, Sophie. Concentrate your energy on that. Everything else can come after."

After he left, she wiped at her eyes. She didn't want Leon to see her wallowing in self-pity. Not with Duncan's death so new. Her father would be grieving hard for him. He had been one of his favorites.

The curtain parted again, and Leon came through; his expression was stoic but his eyes told the truth. She could see the immense sorrow in them.

He stood awkwardly at her bed. "How are you doing?"

"I'm okay. I'll heal."

He lifted his hand as if to touch her leg through the blanket, but lowered it again. It had always been so hard for him to express his emotions. She felt sorry for him that he couldn't grieve the way he should. Raising her hand, she reached for him.

Surprised, he grasped her hand, and she saw that his eyes were wet with unshed tears.

"I'm sorry about Duncan. I know how much he meant to you."

He nodded, pressing his lips together. "We lost another pack member, as well. Bianca. She was so young."

"It could've been a lot worse if Kellen hadn't sensed it in time."

Still gripping her hand in his, Leon glanced over at the next bed where Kellen lay. He stared at him for a few moments, then turned back to Sophie. "He saved your life. And I heard he tried to save Duncan, as well."

"He's a great man."

"I'm beginning to realize that. I'm sorry it comes too late."

More tears trickled down her cheeks. Her emotions were too high to stop them. "It's never too late. When he wakes, you can tell him yourself."

He nodded, but she could tell that he didn't share her optimism about Kellen's fate. "I'll let you sleep." He lifted her hand to his mouth and pressed a kiss to the back, then lowered it to the bed. "I'll come by tomorrow. Sleep and heal, my daughter."

Too choked up to speak, she just nodded. He turned and went to close the curtain separating her and Kellen's beds.

"No. Please leave it open."

He glanced once at Kellen, then back to her. Giving her a small smile, he left her bedside and exited the room.

When he was gone, she wiped her eyes again. He was right, she needed to heal. She couldn't help anyone if she was drowning in her own self-pity in a hospital bed. She had to be strong.

Turning her head to the side, she watched the rise and fall of Kellen's chest; the whooshing sound of his breathing machine was like a nail in her heart. She needed to get strong again. She couldn't help him fight to live if she was weak.

Unfurling her hand from under the blanket, she reached out toward him, her fingers stretching as far as they could go. If only he could feel her, then he would know how much she longed to have him in her arms. Without his touch, she was already starting to grow cold. How long would it take for her heart to freeze solid?

Chapter 28

It was hot and wet in the jungle. The light misting of rain kept everything damp, soggy with warm moisture. With each step Kellen took along the path, mud squelched beneath his boots. Alone he trudged, unsure of where he was headed. But he knew he was waiting for something.

Anticipation reverberated in the warm, humid air.

As he walked, the mournful call of a gibbon pierced the eerie evening silence of the forest. He turned toward the sound, hopeful of getting a glimpse of the agile ape swinging through the trees. But as he moved, another sound echoed behind him.

He swiveled on the path, his heart racing. A lone

shape moved through the fog that enshrouded the jungle. Eyes wide, he watched as a majestic auburn-colored wolf sprang out of the gray mist and padded toward him.

Sophie. She found him at last.

He didn't know how long he'd been waiting for her, but it seemed like a lifetime.

With a stout heart, he waited for her on the path. As she neared, her form started to shift. A set of legs lengthened as another set receded. Her body elongated and the shiny auburn fur disappeared. She was a vision of pale, perfect skin over a long and lithe body. Her long, glorious red hair cascaded over toned shoulders to just cover her rose-tipped breasts.

She took his breath away. He didn't deserve someone as exquisite as Sophie. Noble, remarkable, steadfast Sophie. His Sophie. How did he ever get so lucky?

Smiling, she came to him and wrapped her arms around his neck, pressing the heat of her body against his. When he looked down he noticed that he, too was naked, in the strange way things work in dreams. Because this had to be one. Where else could a reckless man like Kellen be so blessed to be with a woman like Sophie? Surely not in a reality he knew of.

With hands molded to her back, Kellen leaned down and kissed her. Sweeping his tongue between her lips he teased her, reveling in the way she moaned into his mouth. She tasted of the air, and water, the dirt and leaves, everything magical and beautiful about nature.

He ran his hands down her back to the firm swell of her buttocks. Gripping her cheeks, he hauled her up his body. Conjured from his mind, a stone wall appeared behind him and he pressed Sophie against it. Spreading her legs, she wrapped them around his waist, her mouth still feasting on his.

He loved the feel of her in his arms. It felt right, perfect, as if they had been chiseled from the same chunk of stone. If he could have held her like this for the rest of his days he would, but he knew it wasn't to be.

There was something he needed to do first, before forever came.

"My Sophie," he murmured into her neck. The silk strands of her hair brushed his face as he nibbled on her skin. "I've waited so long for you."

"I'm here, Kellen. I'm yours. Tonight, tomorrow, forever."

He cupped her face with his hands. Keeping her gaze, he took her mouth, hard, fast. With a passion he'd never felt before, he nibbled and nipped at her lips and tongue, eager to taste her, eager to take her. A sense of urgency rushed over him—as if these were the last moments of his life.

Sensing his need, Sophie ran a hand between them, and guided his hard length into her. The moment he entered her slick core, a rush of adrenaline and power sizzled through him. With the blast he lost his breath, digging his fingers into her hips to hang on as intense energy pummeled him from the inside out.

She clung to his neck, moaning as he started to thrust in and out. Frantic for her, he drew out then drove in hard and fast, pivoting his hips. She cried out and he covered her mouth with his to swallow it down, to inhale her every wail, every moan of pleasure. He needed to fill himself with her. Only then he knew he'd feel complete, whole. Only then could he truly live.

Kissing her, tasting her, he thrust into her again and again, manic for her. Sounds of their lovemaking echoed around them. The rain had stopped falling, and it was as if they were completely alone, cut off from the rest of the world. It was Sophie and he together, their passion simmering and sparking between them like electricity.

If only they could stay like this forever.

Thighs tightening, gut clenched, Kellen pulled her hips forward as he buried himself deep and found release.

Raking her nails across his back, Sophie writhed against the stone wall, grinding her pelvis into his body. The pleasure was too intense. She couldn't think, it was too much. She'd be lost if she let go. She was afraid.

Even after Kellen orgasmed he continued to move inside her, urging more from her. Shaking her head back and forth, she begged him to stop. "I can't. It's too much."

Kissing away her protests, he ran his hands up to her face. "Just let go, Sophie. Let go and everything will be all right."

She squirmed in his arms, feeling him start to slip away from her. "No. I can't do it. I don't want to."

Smiling, he kissed her again. "You need to let me go." And with that he plunged into her again, and she was lost to her own pleasure. "I'll always come back to you."

In a heated rush she came.

But as soon as she did, Kellen had vanished into the fog.

"Sophie?"

She felt a nudge on her shoulder.

"Wake up."

Startling awake, Sophie sat up in the chair she'd been slouched down in and glanced around, feeling disoriented. Lifting her hands, she noticed the dampness of her skin. She could still smell the rain and the jungle leaves. But it had been a dream, hadn't it?

Gabriel stood at the end of the Kellen's bed watching her. He frowned. "Are you okay? Your eyes were changing."

She nodded as she shifted in the uncomfortable seat. The one she'd been sleeping in for the past two days.

Despite the nurses' protests, she had pushed her hospital bed next to his and held his hand while she slept, and talked to him when she was awake. When one ambitious nurse tried to dissuade her, Sophie had growled so fiercely she actually made the old woman cry and flee in fear.

On the third day, the doctor came and told her that she was being discharged from the hospital. She was healed enough to go home. She told him in no uncertain terms that she was not leaving. They could have their bed back; she'd sleep in the chair.

And that was how Gabriel found her, dozing in the chair, holding on to Kellen's hand.

"I hear they've discharged you."

She stretched her arms and nodded. "Yeah. I'm feeling much better."

"Then what are you still doing here?"

She frowned at him.

"You need to go home and rest, Sophie. You can't fully heal while cooped up in this dreary room. You need some proper food, red meat preferably, some sun, a good night's sleep in a comfortable bed, and you need to go for a long run to work out all your injuries."

He wasn't telling her anything she didn't already know. She just couldn't force herself to leave. What if he woke up and she wasn't here? Or worse, what if her voice and touch were guiding him home, and without them, he gave up and never returned?

"I'll take it under consideration."

He shook his head and yawned. "You're the most stubborn woman I know. And that's saying a lot."

"What about you? What are you doing here? You look like you could use a good twenty-four-hour nap."

"It's been a bad couple of days." He rubbed at his eyes and yawned again.

"I heard about the protest on the television."

"The superintendent is finally putting into place measures to ensure the safety of the humans inside the city. It's going to get uglier before it gets better."

"Did NORM claim responsibility for the attack on the club?"

He nodded. "Just this morning, in a note to the superintendent."

Looking at Kellen, she squeezed his hand tight and rubbed her thumb over his knuckles. "Someone needs to pay for this, Gabe."

"Someone will. Eventually. This group can't hide forever. And when they're found, I promise you I'll be there to take them down."

She glanced at Gabriel. He had a look of fierce determination. She'd known him long enough to know that what he said he meant. She had no doubt that he would take on the terrorist group with his own bare hands if need be. In the past, many people had mistaken Gabriel's calm and logical demeanor as passive. However, the man could be fierce. She'd had the pleasure of seeing him in action.

"Gabe, do you believe in dream projecting?"

He nodded. "I know some vampires can do that. It's an old trick they used to use to seduce their victims."

"I just had a dream about Kellen. I think he's talking to me."

"What's he saying?"

She paused before answering. "To let him go."

He set his hand on her shoulder in that comforting

way of his, and squeezed. "Maybe you should. There's nothing the doctors here can do for him."

Tears rolled down her cheeks. Although it hurt to hear it, Gabriel was right. She couldn't selfishly hold onto him any longer. If it would give him peace, she would let go, however painful it would prove to be.

"Did you bring me the file I wanted?"

Sliding it from under his arm, Gabriel handed it to her without a word. He patted her shoulder again, and then left the room, giving her the privacy she sought.

She returned her attention to Kellen. Still rubbing her thumb over his knuckles, she watched the rise and fall of his chest. She wondered if he could hear her when she spoke to him. Could he feel her caresses? The doctor hadn't been any help in that regard. He couldn't hazard a guess whether Kellen was aware of her or not. His brain was still working. The needle on the EEG was in constant motion, so she knew he was in there struggling to get out.

His body was healing even while he slept. The cuts and bruises on his face, hands and torso were slowly disappearing. So she knew he was still fighting inside.

Leaning over, Sophie set her head onto his chest and listened to his heartbeat. It was strong. He was strong. And she knew he'd come back to her. He had to. She couldn't lose him now, after all they'd been through. After all that he made her feel—the array of emotions and sensations he'd forced from her with his unusual charm and care. She'd never met anyone like

Kellen. He was unique. And she never wanted to be without his distinctiveness. He was special to her and she loved him. It was as simple as that.

And because she loved him so much, there was one more thing she could do for him.

Releasing his hand, she flipped open the file folder and almost instantly found what she was looking for. She dug her cell phone out from her pocket and flipped it open. Hands shaking, she dialed the number.

It rang four times before it was answered. *"Ni hao."*

"Dr. Shen Li? My name is Sophie St. Clair and I'm calling from Nouveau Monde Centre Hospital. There's someone here I think you need to meet."

Chapter 29

The murmuring lycan crowd quieted when Leon stepped into the speaking circle.

Sophie stood on the sidelines, next to her mother, Elsa, and looked over the crowd of two hundred or so seated in the outdoor amphitheater. It never failed to amaze her when the whole pack assembled. For a nonlycan it would certainly be a frightening scene to set eyes upon in one place—all simmering with power, all connected by love and loyalty.

This night they were connected in grief.

It was a full moon, two weeks after Duncan, Cheryl and Bianca's deaths. The pack had gathered to remember them and mourn their loss, as was the tradition.

It had also been two weeks since Kellen was airlifted to China. So Sophie's heart grieved twice as much.

After speaking with Dr. Shen Li on the phone and telling him everything she had learned about Dr. Brenner and the experiments in Vietnam, he agreed to treat Kellen. Sophie had really given him no choice in the matter. She had told him she was sending Kellen to China and that the doctor better be prepared to administer a cure. Even before she had threatened him, the doctor seemed eager to treat Kellen. And it had almost seemed as if he had been waiting for her call.

Two hours later, Sophie, with Gabriel's help, had commandeered transport from the hospital to a facility in Shanghai. She had walked by Kellen's side, still holding his hand, as medics wheeled him down the hall to the elevator that went to the roof of the building, and, finally, to the waiting helicopter. She had kissed Kellen's lips before standing there and watching the transport take off.

She hadn't heard from him, or about him since. And she was going stir crazy.

She hadn't slept well or eaten much in the past fourteen days. Once she was fully healed, she tried to dive back into work at the lab, but found it difficult every time she walked by the workroom and imagined Kellen standing at the table.

At home was no better. Her sheets still carried his scent. As did her skin and her hair. She tried to scrub it away with a loofah sponge, but it only rubbed her flesh raw. His scent had stubbornly remained.

If only she knew he was coming back. Instead, she knew nothing but the pain in her heart.

Dr. Shen Li hadn't returned any of her calls. Every time she called, whether it was day or night, she either reached his answering machine or an assistant that informed her that the doctor was busy and would get back to her. He never did.

It was the not knowing that was destroying her. She didn't know whether to hope or to grieve.

The eerie silence of the crowd brought her back to the service.

Before he began to speak, Leon turned in a circle, looking at each of his pack members. She could sense the expectant edginess of the pack waiting for his words. Leon was revered as pack alpha. He was strong and unbending. He could and would support the weight of the pack's grief on his shoulders.

"Brothers. Sisters." His booming voice echoed throughout the amphitheater. "We gather here today to pay homage to our fallen comrades."

Sophie glanced around and saw varying degrees of sorrow and anger on the faces of her fellow pack members. She matched it with her own.

"Bianca Shaffer was a vibrant young woman with a kind word for everyone she met. She was much too young to die."

"May the moon bless and keep her." The crowd chanted.

"Cheryl McManus was a nurturing and loving woman. A wife and a mother, and a teacher of us all. She will be greatly missed."

"May the moon bless and keep her."

Sophie caught the eye of Cheryl's mate and her heart nearly shattered. Tears streamed down his cheeks as he squeezed his young daughter and son to him. She bit down on her lip to stop her own tears from welling. She could sense their pain. It tore at her throat like claws.

"Duncan Quinn," her father said, and then paused, lowering his head as if to gather his thoughts. Then he raised it and Sophie could see the sheen of tears in his eyes.

His gaze met hers and she smiled at him. He returned her gesture and began again. "Duncan Quinn was a good man. He served this city and his pack well. Not always diplomatic, Duncan was loyal. He loved his pack and would have done anything for it. His death, as well as Bianca's and Cheryl's, will not go unpunished."

"May the moon bless and keep him." The crowd chanted louder, the echo of their collective voices resounding.

Sophie's heart was racing. Her stomach twisted into complicated knots. She couldn't stand it any longer. Surrounded by grief, and anger and love—most of all love—she couldn't stay here in Nouveau Monde and not wither away and die. She had to know about Kellen. She had to know whether he was living or dying. Her heart couldn't stand the pain of it. It would shatter into a thousand pieces.

Glancing around in a panic, she searched for a quiet way out. She knew her father would try to stop her. He could never understand her feelings for Kellen. Not with the pain of Duncan's death still fresh in his heart and mind. She knew he would think that she was betraying her pack by loving Kellen, by leaving them to go to him. But she couldn't deny her heart any longer. It would kill her in the end.

Leon raised his hands up to the sky, toward the full moon radiating her glory on the amphitheater and forest near by. "Now, my friends let us shift and run free with the spirits of our fallen brothers and sisters."

The crowd started to break apart, making room for the task at hand. Some members already started to shift right where they stood into their wolf form.

Before Sophie could move, she felt a presence at her side. A slim hand fit into hers. Turning she looked into her mother's eyes and saw understanding.

"Go to him, Sophie. Do not deny yourself happiness. Not for the pack, not for your father. Follow your heart. It doesn't lie."

Smiling, she hugged her mother tight and inhaled her familiar scent. "Thank you, Mama."

"I love you, daughter." Elsa smoothed her hand down Sophie's head, and then held her back, hands gripping her shoulders. "Now go. I will deal with your father. It's high time I did, anyway."

"I love you, too." She kissed her mother's cheek, then turned to find the easiest way out of the amphitheater without drawing notice to herself.

But before she took three steps, a ripple of tension flowed through the mingling crowd. Lycans who had already shifted were huffing, blowing air out of their nostrils in a sign of heightened anxiety. Others, who had not shifted yet, started to scent the air and jostle from foot to foot nervously.

Pack member looked to pack member, trying to find the source of anxiety. Sophie sensed it, too, but another emotion washed over her. Anticipation. Something was about to happen. She grasped her mother's hand tight and raked her gaze over the crowd, searching for the reason for her awareness.

Near the south entrance of the amphitheater, a great disturbance surged through the crowd. Lycans side-stepped into other lycans, jittery and afraid, making a hole near the gateway. Sophie's gaze settled on the path made in the pack, her heart pounding so hard she could barely breathe.

"Ah, sorry to interrupt," a voice echoed through the theater. A lone figure stepped into the circle, rays of moonlight illuminating his pale face. "But I'm looking for Sophie St. Clair."

Sophie's heart leapt into her throat and she had to swallow down the gasp that threatened to erupt. Her knees wobbled, barely supporting her as she took a few steps forward. Surprised fear gripped her tight. She was afraid that her eyes betrayed her.

She was afraid that if she blinked, Kellen would disappear again.

Chapter 30

As Sophie moved into the pale light cascading over the circle in the stone amphitheater, Kellen nearly dropped to his knees. It felt like he'd been waiting a lifetime to see her again, and he didn't want to wait another single second to have her in his arms.

But he knew he'd have to wait, regardless. The pack wouldn't let her go easily. Especially not Leon. He could already feel the alpha's discontent from across the ring.

When he arrived back in Nouveau Monde he hadn't been thinking clearly. His only thoughts were of Sophie and kissing her. He had gone right from the airport to the lab, searching for her. Olena had told him that

Sophie was at a pack service and told him she probably shouldn't be disturbed, but had given him the address and detailed directions just in case he didn't want to listen to her advice.

She had been right. He wasn't going to listen to anything that kept him from Sophie.

His resolve was steadfast until he had parked his borrowed car and walked half a mile to the meeting place. The energy of over two hundred lycans surged over him, nearly making him wince. He'd never felt anything like it. But still he took the steps toward the entrance. He wouldn't back down now. Not for anything. Not for anyone. He wasn't afraid to live. Not any more.

He wanted Sophie forever, and he wouldn't stop until he had her.

Death tried but failed. A few hundred lycans couldn't be any worse.

Before Sophie could reach him, Leon stepped in her way, effectively blocking her from taking any more steps. Kellen's hands itched to breach the distance between them and touch her. The ache to do so throbbed from the top of his head to his toes.

He glared at Kellen. "How dare you interrupt this grieving service."

Glancing around, Kellen met the gazes—some wolf, some human—of anger—but also of curiosity. "I apologize if my presence insults anyone here. But I'm not leaving. Not without my Sophie."

"*Your* Sophie?" Leon boomed. "I didn't realize that you owned her."

"I don't." He met Leon's piercing gaze, not backing down, not this time. "But she belongs to me, regardless."

"Father," Sophie started.

Leon shook his head. "No. I won't agree to this."

"It's not your choice, Leon, it's Sophie's."

Everyone turned as another woman stepped into the circle next to Leon. From the fiery locks that cascaded around her shoulders, Kellen knew this was Sophie's mother, Elsa.

"This man has not only saved our daughter twice from death, he also risked his own life to try to save Duncan. This man deserves our respect and gratitude, not disdain."

"But he's not a lycan."

Elsa put her hand on Leon's arm. "Does that truly matter, Leon? Would that make him more of an admirable man, worthy of our daughter?"

Leon didn't respond to his wife's words.

Kellen took a step forward. "I love your daughter. I love her more than I can say." He looked at Sophie as he spoke. "She has given me my life back. I can't— *won't*—let you come between us."

At last, Leon's head lifted and he looked at Sophie. "Do you love this man? Would you give up everything you have and everything you are to be with him?"

With tears rolling down her cheeks, she spoke, "Yes. With all my heart, yes."

Nodding, Leon took a step back. "Then I can't stand in your way."

With a gasp of joy, Sophie launched herself at Kellen. He caught her in midair and, hugging her tight, swung her around. His heart thumped so hard he thought it would burst. Closing his eyes, he cradled her close, nuzzling his face into her hair to inhale her intoxicating scent.

She smelled like home. The new one he was hoping to make right now.

"Oh God, I thought I'd never see you again," she murmured as she pressed her lips to the side of his neck.

"I told you I'd always come for you."

"But you were so close to death."

He smiled and kissed her on her cheek. "A minor detail."

He set her on her feet and stared her deep in the eyes. His Sophie. His beautiful lycan. Finally, he found the place he belonged. With her, forever.

"Did the doctor find a cure?" she asked.

"Yes." More tears rolled down her cheeks and he wiped them away with the pads of his thumbs. "I have to go back for more treatments, but the prognosis looks good."

Wrapping her arms around his neck, she hugged him tight. "Oh, Kellen. I thought I lost you."

"Never. Like I said before, I'm here for as long as you want me."

"How about forever?"

Smiling, he covered her mouth with his and whispered, "I wouldn't ask for anything less."

* * * * *

*Celebrate 60 years of pure
reading pleasure with Harlequin®!*

*Step back in time and enjoy a sneak preview
of an exciting anthology from
Harlequin® Historical with*
THE DIAMONDS OF WELBOURNE MANOR

This compelling anthology features three stories
about the outrageous Fitzmanning sisters. Meet
Annalise, who is never at a loss for words… But
that can change with an unexpected encounter in
the forest.

*Available May 2009
from Harlequin® Historical.*

"I'm the illegitimate daughter of notoriously scandalous parents, Mr. Milford. Candidates for my hand are unlikely to be lining up at the gates."

"Don't be so quick to discount your charms, my dear. Or the charm of your substantial dowry. Or even your brothers' influence. There are as many reasons to marry as there are marriages."

Annalise snorted. "Oh, yes. Perhaps I shall marry for dynastic reasons, or perhaps for property or influence. After all, a loveless, practical marriage worked out so well for my mother."

"Well, you've routed me on that one. I can think of no suitable rejoinder." Ned rose to his feet and extended his hand. "And since that is the case, let me be the first to wish you a long and happy spinsterhood."

Her mouth gaped open. And then she laughed.

And he froze.

This was the first time, Ned realized. The first time he'd seen her eyes light up and her mouth curl. The first time he'd witnessed her features melded together in glorious accord to produce exquisite beauty.

Unbelievable what a change came over her face. Unheard of what effect her throaty, rasping laughter had on his body. It pounded a beat upon his ear, quickly taken up by his pulse. It echoed through him, finally residing in his stirring nether regions.

So easily she did it, awakened these sensations within him—without any apparent effort at all. And she had called him potentially dangerous? Clearly the intelligent thing for him to do would be to steer clear, to leave her to the tender ministrations of Lord Peter Blackthorne.

"You were right." She smiled up at him as she took his hand and climbed to her feet. "I do feel better."

Ah, well. When had he ever chosen the intelligent path?

He did not relinquish her hand. He used it to pull her in, close enough that he could feel the warmth of her. "At the risk of repeating Lord Peter's mistake and anticipating too much—may I ask if you'll be my partner in battledore tomorrow?"

Her smiled dimmed. Her breath came a little faster. His own had gone shallow, as if he'd just run a race—and lost. He ran his gaze over the appealing lift of her brow and the curious angle of her chin. His index finger twitched.

"I should like that," she said.

His finger trembled again and he lifted it, traced the pink and tender shell of her ear, the unique sweep of her jaw. Her pulse leaped beneath her skin, triggering his own. Slowly he tilted her chin up, waiting for her to object, to step back, to slap his hand away.

She did none of those eminently sensible things. Which left him free to do the entirely impractical thing.

Baby soft, the skin of her lips. Her whole body trembled when he touched her there.

He leaned in. Her eyes closed, even as she stood straight against him, strung as tight as a bow. He pressed his mouth to hers. It was a soft kiss, sweet and chaste. And yet he was hot and hard and as ready as he'd ever been in his life.

She drew back a little. Sighed. Their breath mingled a moment before she slowly backed away.

"Oh," she breathed. Her dark eyes were full of wonder and something that looked like fear. He took a step toward her, but she only shook her head. His outstretched hand fell to his side as she turned to disappear into the wood. This was the first time, Ned realized. The first time, since he'd come to the house party at Welbourne Manor, that he'd seen her eyes light up.

* * * * *

Follow Ned and Annalise's story
in May 2009 in
THE DIAMONDS OF WELBOURNE MANOR
Available May 2009
from Harlequin® Historical

Available in the series romance section,
or in the historical romance section,
wherever books are sold.

HARLEQUIN
60
YEARS
of pure reading pleasure

We'll be spotlighting a different series
every month throughout 2009
to celebrate our 60th anniversary.

Look for Harlequin® Historical in May!

Celebrations begin with
a sumptuous Regency house party!

Join three scandalous sisters in

THE DIAMONDS OF
WELBOURNE MANOR

Glittering, scintillating, sensual fun
by Diane Gaston, Deb Marlowe
and Amanda McCabe.

60 years of Harlequin,
600 years of romance
in Harlequin Historical!

www.eHarlequin.com   HHBPA09

From acclaimed author

RHYANNON BYRD

Dangerous passions
awaken an ancient hunger
impossible to deny....

April 2009   May 2009   June 2009

Don't miss the debut of
the scintillating *Primal Instinct*
paranormal series
in April 2009!

HQN™

We *are* romance™

www.HQNBooks.com

PHRBT2009

Silhouette **Desire**

MAN of the MONTH

LEANNE BANKS

BILLIONAIRE EXTRAORDINAIRE

Billionaire Damien Medici is determined to get revenge on his enemy, but his buttoned-up new assistant Emma Weatherfield has been assigned to spy on him and might thwart his plans. As tensions in and out of the boardroom heat up, he convinces her to give him the information he needs—by getting her to unbutton a few things....

Available May
wherever books are sold.

www.eHarlequin.com

SD76939

Harlequin® Historical
Historical Romantic Adventure!

If you enjoyed reading
Joanne Rock in the
Harlequin® Blaze™ series,
look for her new book
from Harlequin® Historical!

THE KNIGHT'S RETURN
Joanne Rock

Missing more than his memory,
Hugh de Montagne sets out to find his
true identity. When he lands in a small
Irish kingdom and finds a new liege in the
Irish king, his hands are full with his new
assignment: guarding the king's beautiful,
exiled daughter. Sorcha has had her heart
broken by a knight in the past. Will she be
able to open her heart to love again?

Available April
wherever books are sold.

www.eHarlequin.com   HH29542

You're invited to join our Tell Harlequin Reader Panel!

By joining our new reader panel you will:

- Receive Harlequin® books—they are FREE and yours to keep with no obligation to purchase anything!
- Participate in fun online surveys
- Exchange opinions and ideas with women just like you
- Have a say in our new book ideas and help us publish the best in women's fiction

In addition, you will have a chance to win great prizes and receive special gifts!
See Web site for details. Some conditions apply.
Space is limited.

To join, visit us at
www.TellHarlequin.com.

THBPA0108

REQUEST YOUR FREE BOOKS!

2 FREE NOVELS PLUS 2 FREE GIFTS!

Silhouette®

nocturne™

Dramatic and Sensual Tales of Paranormal Romance.

YES! Please send me 2 FREE Silhouette® Nocturne™ novels and my 2 FREE gifts (gifts are worth about $10). After receiving them, if I don't wish to receive any more books, I can return the shipping statement marked "cancel." If I don't cancel, I will receive 4 brand-new novels every other month and be billed just $4.47 per book in the U.S. or $4.99 per book in Canada, plus 25¢ shipping and handling per book plus applicable taxes, if any*. That's a savings of about 15% off the cover price! I understand that accepting the 2 free books and gifts places me under no obligation to buy anything. I can always return a shipment and cancel at any time. Even if I never buy another book from Silhouette, the two free books and gifts are mine to keep forever.

238 SDN ELS4   338 SDN ELXG

Name	(PLEASE PRINT)

Address	Apt. #

City	State/Prov.	Zip/Postal Code

Signature (if under 18, a parent or guardian must sign)

Mail to the **Silhouette Reader Service:**
IN U.S.A.: P.O. Box 1867, Buffalo, NY 14240-1867
IN CANADA: P.O. Box 609, Fort Erie, Ontario L2A 5X3

Not valid to current subscribers of Silhouette Nocturne books.

Want to try two free books from another line?
Call 1-800-873-8635 or visit www.morefreebooks.com.

* Terms and prices subject to change without notice. N.Y. residents add applicable sales tax. Canadian residents will be charged applicable provincial taxes and GST. Offer not valid in Quebec. This offer is limited to one order per household. All orders subject to approval. Credit or debit balances in a customer's account(s) may be offset by any other outstanding balance owed by or to the customer. Please allow 4 to 6 weeks for delivery. Offer available while quantities last.

Your Privacy: Silhouette is committed to protecting your privacy. Our Privacy Policy is available online at www.eHarlequin.com or upon request from the Reader Service. From time to time we make our lists of customers available to reputable third parties who may have a product or service of interest to you. If you would prefer we not share your name and address, please check here. ☐

SN08R

The Inside Romance newsletter has a NEW look for the new year!

Same great content, brand-new look!

The Inside Romance newsletter is a FREE quarterly newsletter highlighting our upcoming series releases and promotions!

Click on the Inside Romance link on the front page of **www.eHarlequin.com** or e-mail us at insideromance@harlequin.ca to sign up to receive your FREE newsletter today!

You can also subscribe by writing to us at: HARLEQUIN BOOKS Attention: Customer Service Department P.O. Box 9057, Buffalo, NY 14269-9057

Please allow 4-6 weeks for delivery of the first issue by mail.

IRNNEW09

Silhouette®

nocturne™

COMING NEXT MONTH

Available April 28, 2009

#63 CAPTIVE OF THE BEAST • Lisa Renee Jones
Knights of White
Scientist Laura Johnson has a secret—she possesses the
supernatural abilities she studies. Armed with a research
grant, she hopes to find a cure. But when Darkland
Beasts take over her island lab, the only hope she has
of rescue is Rinehart, a Knight of White, who promises
salvation…and delivers passion.

#64 SENTINELS: JAGUAR NIGHT • Doranna Durgin
Sentinels
Sentinel Dolan Treviño is determined to keep
Atrum Core, a community that embraces dark rituals,
from getting its hands on a manuscript of deadly
incantations. The only problem is that the book is on
Meghan Lawrence's ranch—and the last thing she wants
is the help of a shape-shifting jaguar. Can he win her over
to his cause and his heart?

SNCNMBPA0409